"You've b   sir," said Ki...
"Yes," agreed Chakotay,
"a rebel captain of a tiny vessel
that *Voyager* could eat for lunch.
It's not quite the same thing."

Chakotay looked out the shuttle's windows. They had reached *Voyager,* and now the viewscreen was filled with the familiar image of the ship that had been home to him for seven years. As always, he admired her sleek lines, but this time, there was something different.

This time, the ship was his.

Chakotay smiled as he heard a familiar voice. "*Voyager* to Captain Chakotay's shuttle," said Lyssa Campbell. "You are cleared for docking."

Harry smiled a little as well; for seven years, that sort of announcement had been his job.

"*Voyager,* this is Captain Chakotay's party on final approach."

"*Voyager* welcomes you," Campbell replied. "Prepare for docking."

This is the real homecoming, thought Chakotay.

STAR TREK VOYAGER®
OLD WOUNDS

SPIRIT WALK, BOOK ONE

CHRISTIE GOLDEN

Based upon STAR TREK®
created by Gene Roddenberry
and STAR TREK: VOYAGER
created by Rick Berman &
Michael Piller & Jeri Taylor

POCKET BOOKS
New York London Toronto Sydney

This book is a work of fiction. Names, characters, places, and incidents are products of the author's imagination or are used fictitiously. Any resemblance to actual events or locales or persons, living or dead, is entirely coincidental.

An *Original* Publication of POCKET BOOKS

POCKET BOOKS, a division of Simon & Schuster, Inc.
1230 Avenue of the Americas, New York, NY 10020

Copyright © 2004 by Paramount Pictures. All Rights Reserved.

STAR TREK is a Registered Trademark of Paramount Pictures.

This book is published by Pocket Books, a division of Simon & Schuster, Inc., under exclusive license from Paramount Pictures.

All rights reserved, including the right to reproduce this book or portions thereof in any form whatsoever. For information address Pocket Books, 1230 Avenue of the Americas, New York, NY 10020

ISBN: 0-7434-9258-7

First Pocket Books printing November 2004

10 9 8 7 6 5 4 3 2 1

POCKET and colophon are registered trademarks of Simon & Schuster, Inc.

Manufactured in the United States of America

For information regarding special discounts for bulk purchases, please contact Simon & Schuster Special Sales at 1-800-456-6798 or business@simonandschuster.com

*This book is dedicated
to all those who have felt called
to walk a spiritual path.*

Many blessings.

Acknowledgments

Many people were instrumental in the creation of this book. I wish to thank the following individuals: Joe RedCloud, for information on the Lakota language and culture; Malcolm Simpson, M.D., for medical "jargon"; Tom and Amy Gutow, Jeanne Cooper, and Patty Hutchins of Castine, for helping me bring this small Maine town to life in these pages; Mark Anthony for very helpful input at a crucial juncture; and Michael Georges and Robert Amerman, my loyal First Readers.

Any errors contained in this book are entirely my own.

SPIRIT WALK, BOOK ONE

PROLOGUE

2375

THE CARDASSIAN PRISONER of war stretched out on the comfortable Federation bunk, glowered at the uniformed back of the security guard standing outside the force field, and cursed his fortune.

He had been so close. No, not close, he had actually succeeded. If only he'd had more time! So much of what had happened had been just plain bad luck. Timing often was indeed everything, and this time, the timing had been abominable. His colleagues hadn't helped matters any, either. Idiots. Striking that adversarial attitude when, really, they were all on the same side.

But the Cardassian was intelligent enough to realize

that he himself had contributed to his eventual capture. He had been so wrapped up in his work that he'd done some foolish things. Grimacing with embarrassment as he recalled them, he mentally amended that to "stupid" things. Patience was a virtue, a necessity in his work, and he had forgotten that important directive. He had allowed the pressure and the sheer thrill of discovery to push him into making the choices that had led to his present lamentable state.

He sighed, loudly. The guard standing outside his cell shifted her position but didn't look in. At least he wasn't going to be executed, and he had Captain Jean-Luc Picard to thank for that. It had been pleasant, chatting about his work with Picard. The captain had been an attentive, intelligent audience. Perhaps, thought the Cardassian, there was some hope after all. Hope that once the Dominion was victorious, there would be individuals who, although former enemies, would assist in building a new, brighter future.

But at least for now, the Cardassian knew he'd be sitting out the rest of this war. Glancing around at the room that was the brig on a Federation starship, he allowed himself to think that perhaps being a prisoner wouldn't be so bad. Maybe they would let him listen to his beloved opera, or speak with his wife.

Maybe they'd even let him continue his work. After all, the war would eventually be over, and his kind would be needed. Even vital.

*　　*　　*

Commander William Riker glanced at his captain. The patrician features were tight and cold, the hazel eyes blazing with righteous anger, the lips thinned with suppressed outrage. Riker couldn't blame him. He wanted to pop the Cardassian one too.

"At least we got him," he said quietly.

"Hmm? Oh, yes, quite. He can't do any more harm languishing in a Starfleet prison," Picard replied. "Do you know, Number One, I feel a bit queasy simply knowing that he's on my ship."

Riker grinned wickedly. "We'll decontaminate the brig once we've completed the transfer," he joked. He added, more seriously, "I know what you mean. It'll be nice when the bastard's someone else's problem."

"Truer words were never spoken," said Picard.

"Captain," came Data's measured voice, "The *Adventure* is hailing us."

"On-screen," said Picard.

The delicate features of Captain T'Piran filled the screen. The Vulcan woman nodded in recognition.

"Captain Picard. It is pleasant to see you."

"And you, Captain T'Piran. I must confess, I have been eagerly looking forward to your ship's arrival."

She arched a black eyebrow. "I am not surprised," she said. "Your prisoner is . . . distasteful."

Riker chuckled. There was such a thing as an honorable foe, a fellow warrior fighting for a cause he believed in. One could respect such an adversary. But this guy . . .

3

"We are ready to receive the prisoner as soon as you are prepared to transport," T'Piran said.

"Believe me, Captain," Picard replied, "we are more than prepared."

A few moments later, and it was done: the prisoner had been safely transferred to the *Adventure*. Picard and T'Piran exchanged courteous farewells, and when the Vulcan's face was replaced by an image of her small ship leaping into warp, Picard sighed.

"Now, Number One," he said, "About that decontamination you suggested . . ."

With the prisoner safely off the *Enterprise,* the tension aboard the ship dissipated. The Cardassian had been the last reminder of a difficult, though ultimately triumphant, time, and everyone on board was relieved that things were finally getting back to normal. Betazed had been freed. The station the Cardassians had been building was destroyed. Deanna's mother, the irrepressible Lwaxana, and her young son were safe, and a monster was now safely behind a force field aboard the *Adventure*.

To mark the occasion, Riker and Deanna Troi indulged in her favorite decadent pastime—eating chocolate. They met in Ten-Forward as soon as they both went off duty, a few hours after the prisoner had left the ship. Seated at their usual table, Troi lifted the small, dark brown sweet between thumb and forefinger and regarded it with reverence.

"Thalian chocolate," she said in a dreamy voice. "The beans are aged for at least four hundred years." Gesturing with the chocolate for emphasis, she said, "This makes replicated chocolate taste like *targ* dung."

"Huh. Haven't tried *targ* dung in a while," deadpanned Riker. When she offered the candy to him, he declined, saying, "No, thanks. I get more entertainment out of watching you eat it."

She raised an eyebrow and gave him just the hint of a smile. "True connoisseurs consider this an aphrodisiac, you know."

A slow grin spread across Riker's face. "Well, in that case," he amended, leaning forward and opening his mouth.

Suddenly Picard's voice was heard throughout the ship. "All hands, this is the captain. We are at yellow alert. Assume stations and prepare for rescue maneuvers."

They exchanged glances. "You'd think after what we've just been through we'd catch a break," Riker said, rising.

Troi popped the last of the exquisite chocolates into her mouth. Around the confection, she said, "We never catch breaks, Will. Haven't you figured that out by now?" And they headed for the turbolift.

Picard glanced up as they entered the bridge. Riker didn't like the look on his face. As he and Troi assumed their seats, Riker asked, "Status?"

"We've received a distress call from the *Adventure,*"

Picard said grimly. "They were seconds away from a warp core breach and attempting to evacuate when they sent the call. We heard nothing more. Presently we are heading to their last known location at warp nine."

Their eyes met. Both men knew that even warp ten, if such a thing were possible, might not be fast enough. Seconds—sometimes nanoseconds—counted. If you weren't able to shut down a warp core breach in time, chances were you wouldn't make it to the escape pods.

Their fears were confirmed when they dropped out of warp. There was no sign of a ship, no sign of escape pods—nothing but debris floating in the iciness of space.

Just to be sure, Picard asked in a clipped voice, "Deanna? Anything?"

Her large brown eyes full of sorrow, she shook her head. "No one survived, Captain."

Riker hated moments like these—moments when he was utterly helpless and there was no action to take to ease the pain. The *Adventure* was no more; Captain T'Piran, her five-member crew, and their infamous prisoner were dead.

"When we first brought Crell Moset on board," said Picard, "I assured him he wouldn't be killed."

Riker gazed out at the floating debris. "Looks like you lied."

Chapter

1

ADMIRAL KATHRYN JANEWAY APPROACHED the pool table, her jaw set, her eyes bright. Captain Chakotay thought Joan of Arc might have worn that same look of passionate determination, gripping a lance instead of a cue stick. Janeway surveyed the table, called her shot, lined it up, and to the surprise of neither of her watching friends, sank the ball.

The three of them were in the real, bona fide Sandrine's in Marseilles. Lieutenant Commander Tom Paris had made the introductions a few months ago and told Sandrine about how popular the replicated bistro was on *Voyager*'s holodeck. Sandrine had been enormously pleased to think that her "simple, *petit bistro* offered so much comfort to lost travelers." The elegant blond proprietor had kissed everyone on the cheek—the men on each cheek, a bit too lingeringly—and offered complimentary champagne and caviar all around.

Tonight, six months after *Voyager*'s return home, only Janeway, Chakotay, and Dr. Jarem Kaz were enjoying the dim lighting and cozy atmosphere of the bistro. Janeway sipped a glass of fine French wine between shots, Kaz had indulged in Antarean brandy, and Chakotay held a glass of cold mineral water with lime.

"Got a big day tomorrow," he said as he ordered, "and besides, I have to stay sharp if I have any hope of winning against Admiral Shark here."

In the end, though, Chakotay realized that his decision to stick to water didn't help much. Janeway continued to dominate the game.

"Maybe we should change the rules," Kaz said to Chakotay as Janeway sank her fourth ball.

Janeway looked up in mock horror. "Gentlemen, I'm surprised at you. You should know by now that I never, *ever* change or bend rules."

The two men exchanged amused glances. Chakotay had been Janeway's first officer for seven years and knew nearly everything there was to know about the woman who had brought her crew home against impossible odds. Janeway kept to the spirit of the law, but not always the letter. She took risks and followed her gut instincts and her heart's advice as well as the logic of her brain.

Sometimes those risks didn't pay off. Sometimes they exacted a dreadful toll. But most of the time, Kathryn Janeway won.

Just as she was doing now.

Kaz had known Janeway and Chakotay for only a few months, but the three of them had become fast friends in that time. The Trill doctor had risked everything to help them stop a deadly threat to Earth shortly after the *Voyager* crew had returned home. During that crisis, Kaz had trusted Janeway as Chakotay had learned to trust her, with much less reason. And with that trust, he had earned two friends for life.

There were other reasons why Chakotay found himself gravitating to the doctor. The Trill's previous host, Gradak, had been a Maquis, something he and Chakotay had in common. Gradak Kaz had died shortly after the devastating sneak attack on Tevlik's moon base—the very site out of which Chakotay himself had operated during the war. As Chakotay had once told Janeway, if his ship hadn't been spirited away to the Delta Quadrant by the Caretaker, he would probably have died on Tevlik's moon along with several thousand other Maquis and their entire families.

Even more significantly, both Gradak and Chakotay had personally known the traitor Arak Katal, the Bajoran who had betrayed the Maquis to the Cardassians and was directly responsible for the massacre.

Chakotay liked Jarem for himself, never having

known Gradak. But the knowledge that part of his new friend understood what it meant to be Maquis made Chakotay even more inclined to befriend the Trill.

As much as he personally liked Kaz, he respected him even more. The Trill had been Chakotay's first choice to replace the Doctor on board *Voyager*. Kaz had readily agreed, and Chakotay was looking forward to working with him.

"Oh, come on," sputtered Kaz as Janeway prepared to sink yet another ball.

The outburst was perfectly timed. Janeway laughed and her shot went wild. Still laughing, she yielded to Chakotay.

"I pass it to you, my old friend," she said, and he knew she referred to more than the table.

Tomorrow would mark his first official day as captain of the *U.S.S. Voyager*. The ship would be relaunched, with its new captain, new crew, and new missions. It was a bittersweet moment for Chakotay.

"Six, right-hand side pocket," he said, and lined up the shot.

Janeway had always told him the truth, and she'd been frank about how hard it had been for her to persuade some in Starfleet Command to award Chakotay the position of captain. He'd found out later just how hard she'd argued.

"You should have seen her, Chakotay," Admiral Kenneth Montgomery, former foe and now friend, said to him one night not too long ago. "I'll be frank—it ought to have been impossible. You were a Maquis, and the only proof they had that you could be trusted was her word and *Voyager*'s logs. But Janeway wasn't going to leave the room until she'd gotten you that captaincy. I've never seen anyone argue so passionately for something in my entire life. By the time she was done, I think everyone was prepared to offer you the presidency of the Federation."

Chakotay found out later that others, too, had come before Starfleet Command to speak to his accomplishments—Montgomery among them. He'd blushed to hear how highly thought of he was among both relative strangers and his former crewmates. Chakotay knew he'd been given a rare opportunity, and he was determined that his friends—especially Kathryn—would never regret their decision to support him.

He'd also been allowed to assemble what he considered to be a "dream crew," the finest from *Voyager* and some of the best the Federation could offer in the Alpha Quadrant.

In addition to Kaz, he'd been able to get Harry Kim to agree to take over security, Lyssa Campbell, *Voyager*'s former transporter officer, to step into Harry's old position at ops, and the unwittingly entertaining and intelligent Vorik as chief engineer. Two amazing women as pilot and science officer and a Huanni counselor—every captain's first choice for that important, delicate, and sometimes difficult job—rounded out the senior staff.

"You're sure you don't want to work as a team, Kaz?" Chakotay asked as he lined up his second shot. "It might take both of us to beat her."

"No, I'll wait and play the admiral—I mean, whoever wins this game," said Kaz.

"Yeah, yeah, wait until you're on my ship, my friend," said Chakotay. He missed the next shot, and Kaz looked at him meaningfully.

Chakotay drank some of his water and looked around. Sighing, he said, "This is almost a perfect evening. I only wish Tom were here."

Janeway, chalking her cue, gave him a sympathetic glance. She knew he was referring to more than just the evening's entertainment.

"We tried," she said.

"I know," he replied. "Two black sheep was just too much for Starfleet to swallow."

"For right now," Janeway said. "Thirteen, corner pocket. And besides, he's still on parental leave on Boreth, with B'Elanna and Miral." Before she shot, she regarded Chakotay intently. "Don't worry, Chakotay. I've got my eye on Tom. I'm not going to let Starfleet forget about him. He's too valuable an officer."

Chakotay had wanted Tom Paris as his first officer. Despite—or perhaps because of—their clashes in earlier years, Paris was someone he had learned to trust completely. It had seemed so right, so logical a choice, that even now the memory of Janeway gently telling him that his request had been denied stung.

"They're willing to gamble on you, and they're willing to gamble on Tom," Janeway had said. "Just not both of you on the same ship."

"We were on the same ship for seven years," Chakotay had said angrily. "We did a pretty good job then."

It was at that point Janeway had revealed to him how hard she had fought to get him *Voyager*'s captaincy . . . and had revealed the compromise she'd been forced to make.

"But it's adding insult to injury," said Kaz, referring to that compromise. Clearly his mind was running along the same path as Chakotay's. "I mean, not only did they refuse to let Tom back on *Voyager* as your first officer, but they foisted Priggy on you."

Once again, Janeway's shot went wild as she choked with laughter. "Kaz, I'm beginning to think this is deliberate," she remonstrated. Sobering, she said, "It's a good thing none of us is on duty right now or I'd have to reprimand you for that comment. Andrew Ellis is a sterling Starfleet officer. He's highly decorated and long overdue for a first officer position. You're lucky to have him, Chakotay, and I know he's very much looking forward to serving with you."

"Everything you said is completely true," Chakotay agreed. "And so is the nickname." He stepped into position and made his shot.

"He's not a prig," said Janeway, sounding unconvinced herself. "He's just . . . a touch conservative." She paused. "And by-the-book."

CHRISTIE GOLDEN

"And far too stuffy for a thirty-year-old," said Kaz.

Janeway glanced from one man to the other. "Somehow I think you and Chakotay will loosen him up a bit."

"It's not Ellis himself I mind," said Chakotay, amending immediately, "Okay, at least not much. I just feel like Starfleet wants him to be my nanny."

"Who knows," mused Kaz. "Maybe beneath that starched uniform beats the wild heart of an untamed rebel."

Chakotay came dangerously close to snorting his water. "Damn it, Kaz," he sputtered. All three of them were laughing now.

"All right," Janeway said, mirth still bubbling in her voice. "No more comments about Commander Ellis. He's got the credentials and you're to give him a fair shot, both of you. Agreed?"

"Yes, ma'am," said Chakotay obligingly, knowing the term annoyed her.

She glared at him. "Changing the subject," she said, "I want to make sure you know that after the initial resistance, I've been hearing a lot of enthusiasm about your taking over *Voyager.* In fact, you were specifically requested for this mission."

Chakotay was so surprised by this comment that he missed the shot. He was sure that unlike Kaz, who made every wry comment with deliberate calculation, Janeway hadn't timed her statement purposely to throw his game off.

"Really?" he said. "Considering the nature of the mission, that surprises me."

"It shouldn't," Janeway said. "It's just one of those little ironies that make life so interesting. The odds that your first mission would take you back to areas of space that you fought to liberate as a Maquis might seem steep until you consider that nearly everything right now is revolving around recovering from the war."

"The war we missed," said Chakotay. "I'm tired about hearing how lucky we were."

Janeway had just two more balls to sink before she won the game. She examined the table as she spoke.

"The fact that you're involved in this right now indicates that everyone is ready to move into the healing phase," she said.

"Not everyone," said Kaz. "I have to tell you, as someone who was here when the war was going on, that the last thing anyone expected was to have some of the worlds we fought to protect turn on us afterward."

Janeway made her shot. Only one ball was left on the table.

"I wouldn't say they turned on us," she said mildly. "The war was dreadful. We lost so many people. Some planets are inclined to blame Federation policy instead of the Dominion for those losses. It's to be expected." She sank the final ball with a great deal of force. "But it's not correct."

"The Federation has always been about reaching out to others, helping them," said Kaz. "Being involved, being compassionate. Just because sometimes some worlds or species take advantage of that doesn't mean the policy doesn't work. In the history of the Federation, that policy has worked much, much more often than it's failed."

"I couldn't agree more," said Janeway, racking the balls for the next game. She handed her cue to Kaz. "Of course, every Federation planet has the right to withdraw from the Federation if it so chooses. But it's important that that choice be made for the right reasons, or everyone suffers."

"The galaxy is smaller than ever these days," said Chakotay. "We've expanded into two more quadrants in just the last few years. No one can afford to go it alone."

Chakotay knew that this theme of unity had become Janeway's passion over the last few months. While she still enjoyed teaching the fresh faces at the Academy with Tuvok, it wasn't enough to keep her sharp mind occupied. As a captain, she might have been able to scratch the itch by taking her ship out to where the action was. As an admiral, she didn't have that opportunity.

But she had something else, Chakotay had learned: access to information, and power to directly influence policy. The thing that had kept *Voyager* together under remarkable circumstances for seven full years was the crew's devotion to Federation ideals, even—perhaps especially—on the part of the Maquis among them. To come home to a shattered quadrant recovering from war, and to see the Federation starting to splinter because of it, had been particularly painful to Janeway, and she had volunteered to take under her wing any and all missions that kept the still-wounded Federation together.

Kaz broke, and they were all quiet for a moment as they watched the balls roll to various positions on the table.

"Two, side pocket," Kaz said.

An unpleasant thought occurred to Chakotay. "Did Starfleet Command assign me this mission as a test? To remind me of my place?"

As soon as he spoke the words, he realized how childish they sounded. But Janeway didn't appear surprised.

"That had occurred to me too," she said. "I think it's a by-product of the cynicism we experienced when we first returned. But no, Chakotay, I don't think that's truly the case. You're taking passengers to repopulate Loran II. The fact that this planet has a similar history to Dorvan V was definitely taken into consideration, certainly. How could it not be? I don't think anyone wanted to rub your nose in anything. On the contrary, the comment I've heard is that you were the best man for the job because you had empathy for the colonists, a sort of empathy no one else possessed. They, too, were handed over to the Cardassians; they, too, had to make the painful choice between evacuation and staying. In a mission all about healing and recovery, that sort of a connection is a big thing."

She smiled gently at him. A muffled oath from Kaz made them glance at the table. The Trill glumly handed Janeway the cue.

"Next time," he grumbled, "we play poker."

Chapter 2

CHAKOTAY HAD ALWAYS HAD a fierce loyalty to his friends, and his time on *Voyager* had only strengthened that quality. So when the small group gathered in the private room on Earth Station McKinley burst into applause when he entered in full dress uniform, he could honestly say that there wasn't anyone there he hadn't spent time with recently.

He was a little embarrassed at the effusiveness of the greeting. Holding up his hands, he said, "Thank you, everyone. I'm so pleased you could attend. This is a very special moment for me, and I can't think of a better way to celebrate it than with all of you. Please," he said, gesturing to the holographic waiters serving champagne and appetizers, "as you were."

Laughter rippled throughout the crowd as Chakotay greeted his friends one by one. Janeway was there, of course, beaming with pride. They embraced affectionately, and Chakotay kissed her cheek.

Commander Tuvok stood by her side. Like everyone else, he had applauded politely, but he looked as though he regarded such an effusive display of approbation beneath him. Chakotay smothered a grin as he shook the Vulcan's hand.

"It's not going to be the same without you as head of security, Tuvok," Chakotay said.

Tuvok inclined his head graciously at the compliment. "Thank you, Captain. However, I trust Lieutenant Kim will serve you admirably."

"I trust so, too," said Lieutenant Harry Kim. He was present at this gathering because he would be the one taking Chakotay to the ship later. Everyone else under Chakotay's command was already aboard *Voyager.*

"Com—" Harry blushed. "Excuse me, *Captain*— you remember Libby Webber?"

"It would be hard to forget someone like you, Miss Webber," said Chakotay, turning to greet the lovely young musician who was famous throughout the quadrant. "It's a pleasure to see you again."

"Thank you, Captain. I'm honored to be here today," Libby smiled.

Not for the first time, Chakotay thought Harry Kim a lucky man. His family was alive and well, he was progressing steadily in a career he loved, and he was dating a woman who was as intelligent and talented as she was attractive. Clearly, they doted on one another.

"Sorry to be taking Harry away from you again," Chakotay said.

"As long as it's not another seven years, I'll be fine," she replied, giving him a broad, sweet smile.

Chakotay lifted his eyes from Libby's to gaze right into a pair of intelligent blue ones. A slow smile spread across his face as he took the woman's hand.

"Hello, Seven," he said softly.

She smiled in return, that deep, radiant smile that reached her eyes and made everyone who saw it realize with certainty that she was human now, no longer Borg. They had seen one another a few times as friends since she had ended their relationship at their welcome-home banquet, and things had been easier than he had expected. Seven's new job in the Federation think tank had been enough of a challenge to stimulate her powerful intellect, and her aunt Irene had exerted a warmly humanizing influence. The result was that Seven of Nine seemed happier than Chakotay had ever seen her on *Voyager*.

He recalled the fears that she had expressed, fears that, if truth be told, he had shared to some degree. She had worried that she would not fit in on Earth. And those fears had appeared to be borne out initially. Now, those unpleasant events were but a memory, and Seven of Nine had blossomed under the blue skies of Earth.

"Congratulations, Captain Chakotay," she said,

squeezing his hand. "Your promotion is well deserved. Your crew is to be envied."

"Thanks," he said. "Where's that attractive aunt of yours?"

"Right here," came Irene Hansen's warm voice. He turned and found himself caught up in a tight embrace, complete with a big kiss on the cheek. "You were so sweet to include me in the invitation!"

"Of course I included you," he said. He winked and added, "I've had too many delicious meals at your house not to hedge my bets for more."

A heavy sigh made him turn around. The Doctor was regarding one of the holographic waiters with a sad look on his face. Chakotay felt a pang of sympathy. The Doctor had unwittingly gotten himself embroiled in controversy when he arrived on Earth. While he had been cleared to Starfleet's satisfaction, Chakotay knew he was still passionate about holographic rights. The waiters that had been programmed to cater to the needs of the guests at this small party were hardly the remarkable holographic program that the Doctor was, but Chakotay knew the Doctor felt a sort of kinship with them nonetheless.

"All ready for your presentation, Doc?" Chakotay inquired. The Doctor had been invited to speak before a special Federation subcommittee on the issue of holographic rights. Chakotay knew how important this was to the Doctor, but suspected that it was rather low on the list of the Federation's priorities. He hoped he was mistaken and that the Doctor's comments would be well received.

The Doctor turned and brightened when he saw Chakotay. "Captain Chakotay! It's such a pleasure to be here on this auspicious day. Thank you for asking. Yes, I'm a bit nervous about it, but Seven assures me that my speech is powerful and compelling." He hesitated, and then added, "Of course, she's listened to me read it six times now."

"It is a strong and well-reasoned piece of oratory, Doctor," said Seven, "but repetition does dull one's appreciation for it."

"I wish it had been possible to have the two of you back on *Voyager*," Chakotay said sincerely. "We could certainly use you. But it seems to me that both of you are enjoying your present line of work. Is that the case?"

"It is . . . stimulating," said Seven.

"What exactly is it you think about in your think tank?"

"Everything," the Doctor replied.

"The Doctor exaggerates," Seven chided.

"Not by much," the Doctor retorted.

"Our think tank serves the Federation in general, not one specific branch. Therefore, we are not inhibited by which lines of inquiry and investigation we choose to pursue. Our requests for supplies and information are met without complaint. We analyze the potential flaws in military plans, search for cures for diseases, and test inventions. We exchange views, perform research, conduct experiments, and then present our findings to the Federation."

"Only Seven could make such thrilling work sound dull," said the Doctor. "There are eight of us, each one a specialist in his or her—or its—field. We bounce ideas off each other. Brainstorm. Approach things from off-the-wall directions." His eyes gleamed. "Sometimes we just flat-out argue."

"We do not argue," said Seven in a tone of voice that indicated they'd hashed this one out before. "We debate. There is a difference."

"Seven," said the Doctor patiently, "*food* was thrown yesterday. Hurling of victuals does not constitute proper terms of debate."

"That has never happened before, and Tklish expressed proper remorse and chagrin," said Seven. She turned to Chakotay and arched an eyebrow. "We debate," she repeated.

Chakotay's smile grew as a comforting warmth stole over him. He loved listening to these two banter with each other. It was so good to be back in the company of these dear old friends. Almost all of them were here. Even Neelix had sent him a message of congratulations last night all the way from the Delta Quadrant. While Chakotay was silently grateful that the Talaxian's longing to personally cater the party was impossible to fulfill, Neelix's chipper presence would have been deeply welcomed.

The soft sound of a youngster clearing her throat

drew his attention back to the room. He turned and saw Naomi Wildman grinning at him. Behind her stood the girl's parents, the Ktarian Greskrendtregk and the human Samantha Wildman, and Icheb.

"Now this is a surprise," Chakotay said to Icheb. "You're supposed to be in classes, aren't you?"

"When your instructors are Admiral Janeway and Commander Tuvok," Icheb replied, "it's a little easier to skip class for *Voyager*'s relaunch."

"I imagine it would be." Chakotay shook the former Borg's hand and clapped him on the back. He opened his arms and hugged Naomi. "Goodness, Naomi, you've grown so much!"

"In a year or so I'll be able to apply for Starfleet Academy," said Naomi, looking more like a coltish teenager than the appealing little girl Chakotay remembered.

"Time does fly," said Chakotay. "What field would you be interested in pursuing?"

Naomi looked thoughtful. "I'm not quite sure yet. Either quantum mechanics theory or mythology and culture. Or maybe genetics."

"That's quite a variety of interests. Whichever you pick, I'm sure you'll do your parents proud," Chakotay said. Looking at her mother, he added, "Congratulations, by the way, on your promotion, Lieutenant."

"Thank you, sir," said Samantha Wildman formally before breaking into her easy grin. Chakotay exchanged pleasantries with Greskrendtregk, then continued to greet his guests.

If only Tom and B'Elanna had been able to attend, the circle of companions would be complete. But the Paris family was on Boreth. After B'Elanna had undergone a traumatic ordeal in an attempt to find her mother, she discovered a need to immerse herself in Klingon tradition for a time. Tom, a full-blooded human, had been permitted to reside in the sacred place only after special dispensation from Emperor Kahless himself, and it would have insulted the famous Klingon honor to request permission to leave for anything less than a death in the family—and, Chakotay mused wryly, knowing Klingons, perhaps not even then.

He wandered around for a while, permitting himself to enjoy the moment. All too soon his attention was directed back to his duties by a soft cough from Kim.

"Captain," Kim said, "we should be departing shortly."

"Of course," said Chakotay. Janeway had been watching him without appearing to do so, and now she stepped forward.

"Everyone have a glass of something?" she asked, smiling a little as Seven took a glass of apple juice instead of champagne. The former Borg did not handle alcohol well. "I would like to propose a toast."

Janeway turned to Chakotay, her blue eyes sparkling like the champagne she lifted in his honor.

"To Captain Chakotay," she said, her voice trembling ever so slightly. "The best first officer anyone could ever have, and a captain who will do Starfleet proud. If I could make one wish for you, Captain Chakotay, it would be that you have a crew on *Voyager* who serves you as well as mine served me."

"Three cheers for Captain Chakotay!" said Harry Kim. Chakotay blushed at the old custom. "Hip hip—"

"Hooray!" everyone chorused.

Twice more Kim led the cheers and then the guests broke into applause. Chakotay waved, calling for silence.

"It really is good to see so many of you," he said. "I hope I will indeed do Starfleet proud. After all," he added, "I did learn from the best. I've got a toast of my own. To the former captain of this noble ship—Admiral Kathryn Janeway!"

They toasted Janeway and drank. After a few sips, Chakotay returned his half-finished flute to the serving tray.

"Time to go on duty," he said.

The quick shuttle ride to the ship, a tradition held over from the times when transporter technology was iffy at best, was a pleasant one. Kim and Chakotay were at ease with one another and felt no need to make small talk. Chakotay was looking forward to greeting—and in some cases, meeting—the rest of *Voyager*'s crew.

His crew.

Kim looked up from piloting the shuttlecraft. He smothered a grin.

"Nervous, Captain?"

"A bit," Chakotay admitted. "It's not every day you get your first command."

"But you've been captain before, sir," said Kim.

"Yes," agreed Chakotay, "a rebel captain of a tiny vessel that *Voyager* could eat for lunch. It's not quite the same thing. Changing the subject," he said meaningfully, "how are the passengers doing?"

"They boarded about an hour ago. Commander Ellis showed them to their quarters. They have been informed that Astall is happy to talk with them when they feel up to it, and that we'll be picking up a spiritual advisor as well."

"If they don't take advantage of Astall's counsel on their own, I may have to nudge them to do so," said Chakotay. He still couldn't believe his good luck in getting a Huanni counselor.

Over a hundred years ago, when the Huanni first joined the Federation, they acquired a slightly tongue-in-cheek reputation for being the antidote to the Vulcans. Whereas Vulcans prized control over their emotions, the Huanni honored and encouraged expression of theirs. Many in Starfleet wondered if they'd ever temper themselves sufficiently to interact appropriately with less . . . enthusiastic species, but those fears proved to be groundless. After about twenty years of exposure to others, the Huanni were able to modify their behavior. They were still highly emotional, but most were quite capable of controlling themselves when they needed to.

The revered ambassador Skalli Jksili, the first Huanni to graduate from Starfleet Academy, had been the bridge between her species and many others. After an incident with the famous Captain James T. Kirk, during which she had helped to reunite two estranged peoples, Skalli strode boldly into Federation legend. It was she who had first suggested that Huanni might be valuable counselors, provided they were properly trained in interacting with humans and other Federation member species.

It had been a stroke of brilliance. The Huanni were capable of profound empathy and sympathy, to the point of completely immersing themselves in another's torment. While such deep involvement was not advisable for humans, as it caused undue and sometimes dangerous stress, the Huanni thrived on it. The chemicals such feelings released strengthened their immune systems and in general improved their health. In return, they were able to provide their patients with a sincere, compassionate presence. When this natural empathy was combined with more traditional counseling methods, the result was positive for everyone. Captains clamored for them, but there were too few to meet the demand. Chakotay suspected that Janeway had, again, pulled a few strings for him. He was looking forward to meeting Astall, as well as others.

He looked out the shuttle's windows. They had reached *Voyager,* and now the viewscreen was filled with the familiar image of the ship that had been home to him for seven years. As always, he admired her sleek lines, but this time, there was something different.

This time, the ship was his.

Chakotay smiled as he heard a familiar voice. "*Voyager* to Captain Chakotay's shuttle," said Lyssa Campbell. "You are cleared for docking."

Harry smiled a little as well; for seven years, that sort of announcement had been his job.

"*Voyager*, this is Captain Chakotay's party on final approach."

"*Voyager* welcomes you," Campbell replied. "Prepare for docking."

This is the real homecoming, thought Chakotay.

Chapter

3

THE SHUTTLE DOOR OPENED, and Kim stepped out first. The young lieutenant stood straighter than Chakotay had ever seen him, and he looked very serious.

"Captain on deck!" Kim announced.

Chakotay heard the high piping sounds, and everyone snapped to attention. He strode to the podium that had been set up, his eyes flickering over the assembled crowd. He caught the gazes of Kaz, Lieutenant Lyssa Campbell, Lieutenant Vorik. Kaz winked, ever so subtly, and smiled a little. Chakotay resisted the impulse to wink in return.

Commander Andrew Ellis, *Voyager*'s new first officer, stood ramrod straight. Chakotay took in the impeccable dress uniform, the regulation-trimmed mustache, the thinning hair, and the pale blue eyes, and sighed inwardly.

Chakotay produced a small padd, cleared his throat, and began to read the formal letter that officially granted him command of the ship he so loved.

"You are hereby requested and required to take command of the *U.S.S. Voyager* as of this date. Signed, Admiral Kathryn Janeway, Starfleet Command."

The words never varied. It felt good to be part of a tradition. This was something that his "contrary" nature yearned for every now and then.

Impulsively, Chakotay put the padd down and said, "As everyone here knows, I served on this ship as its first officer for seven years. It's good to be back, and also rather humbling. I'm looking forward to seeing where the new voyage takes us all."

Leaving the podium, he stepped forward to greet his crew, beginning with his first officer.

"Commander Ellis," he said formally, shaking his first officer's hand. "Good to see you again."

"Thank you, sir. It is an honor to serve."

"How are our passengers?"

"Very well, sir. Per regulations, I have confined them to quarters until your arrival."

Chakotay tried to hide his surprise and disappointment. He leaned in closer and spoke quietly, trying not to embarrass Ellis.

"In the future, I'd appreciate it if you came to me first before assuming that all regulations apply to all our guests," he said. Ellis's face twitched slightly. Chakotay added, "Come by my ready room and we'll have a little chat once we're under way."

"Of course, sir. My apologies, sir."

"You did nothing wrong, Commander. It's just . . . as a captain I'm a little more relaxed than you might be used to."

Something glimmered in Ellis's pale blue eyes, then disappeared. Disapproval. Chakotay couldn't help but wonder for the hundredth time how he and his very different first officer would manage to get along.

"Vorik," said Chakotay more loudly, moving on to his chief engineer. "I'm sure you're delighted to be back on familiar turf. Only B'Elanna Torres knows that engine room better than you."

Vorik inclined his head at the compliment. "I can only strive to emulate Lieutenant Commander Torres."

"You probably won't have as difficult a time restraining your desire to punch someone when things go wrong," Chakotay joked, enjoying Vorik's raised eyebrow. He was even more fun to tease than Tuvok.

"I trust not, Captain." The Vulcan sounded slightly shocked. Chakotay smothered a grin.

Kaz was next. They shook hands and exchanged formal pleasantries, but Chakotay was more interested in greeting the tall, attractive woman who was standing next to the Trill doctor. She had rich brown skin and long, glossy black hair tied back in a ponytail. He could tell she had muscles beneath the uniform, and she held her head proudly, almost defiantly.

"Lieutenant Akolo Tare," he said, recognizing her from her holophoto. "I'm glad to finally meet you in person."

She took his hand. Her grip was firm, no nonsense, and she met his gaze evenly. "Likewise, Captain."

"You came highly recommended," he said. "I only regret that you and *Voyager*'s former pilot can't swap stories."

"Thank you, sir. But I'm a pilot, not a storyteller. I must admit, though, I am looking forward to getting my hands on the famous *Delta Flyer*."

"Alas, you'll have to wait. They're still tinkering with it."

A flash in those dark eyes. "Let us hope," she said, "they don't tinker too much."

"Lieutenant," he said thoughtfully, "I think we'll get along just fine."

Chakotay recalled her bio. Tare was of Polynesian descent and had fought in the Dominion War. She had been awarded the Grankite Order of Tactics and the Starfleet Citation for Conspicuous Gallantry for various actions performed during that conflict. But what concerned him the most was something that had happened to her recently.

Six months ago, Tare had had the misfortune of being one of several Starfleet officers who had been abducted by the overly zealous Oliver Baines, the man who had inspired the so-called HoloRevolution. She, along with several others, had been trapped in a brutal holographic simulation meant to demonstrate how demeaning such recreation was to the holograms. According to witnesses, Tare had been literally carried off, thrown across a saddle like a sack of goods, when she dared to stand up to Baines's bullies.

After she returned to duty, her commanding officer was worried about her. He had noted his concerns in her bio, with mentions of "erratic behavior" and her own request for a transfer. But Tare could give Tom Paris a run for his money in the piloting department, and Chakotay wasn't going to hold anyone's past against him or her.

Chakotay turned to the woman standing beside Tare. Both women had dark skin and shiny black hair, but there the resemblance ended. Devi Patel, who had a wealth of knowledge about all things scientific, was not a large person to begin with, and standing next to the Amazonian Tare, she looked even more petite. But her reputation was equal to the pilot's.

"Welcome, Lieutenant Patel," Chakotay said warmly. "Your reputation precedes you."

"As, of course, does yours, Captain," she replied. Her hand was tiny in his grasp, but firm, and her eyes were bright and intelligent. With her short-cropped black hair, she looked almost Vulcan.

He turned at last to greet his counselor. Chakotay, like many humans, found the Huanni very pleasant to look at. Their females were usually as tall as a typical human man, the males even taller, but very slender, and they moved in a graceful manner. The word "willowy" came to mind. Their skin was pale purple, their hair a deeper shade of that color, and they had ears that resembled a kangaroo's. It used to be that you could tell the emotions of a Huanni simply by the ear position, but that wasn't true any longer. Over time, they'd developed what he'd heard them call "Federation ears," and now kept their telltale appendages in a neutral position unless they were extremely agitated.

Astall stood properly at attention, her "Federation ears" in place, but her eyes were shining and her mouth curved up just a bit too much for a formal situation. Chakotay had no doubt that if they had been alone, the counselor would have given him an enormous hug. But she didn't do so here. Instead, she extended a long-fingered hand.

"Lieutenant Astall," he said warmly. "I was so pleased to hear you'd been assigned to *Voyager*. We're extremely lucky to have you."

Her large eyes twinkled, but her voice was calm. "Thank you, Captain. I am looking forward to serving."

Chakotay turned to the next person in line. "Lieutenant Campbell," he said to the attractive blond woman standing next to the Huanni. "How very good to see you again."

Lyssa Campbell smiled, and her eyes sparkled.

"Likewise, sir. I'm looking forward to being a member of your bridge crew."

"Much better than being stuck down alone in the transporter room, I'd think," Chakotay replied, and Lyssa's normally porcelain cheeks colored. A vivacious woman who thrived in the company of others, she'd been notorious for complaining about how isolating a job being the transporter chief had been.

"Well, sir," she said gamely, "the company will be a lot better."

Chakotay continued to move down the receiving line, greeting crew members both old and new. At last, he had spoken to them all. He wished it were possible for him to meet every single crew member on his ship. During his seven years on *Voyager,* he had come to know everyone very well indeed. It was strange, having to maintain a distance now. He hoped that he could emulate his former captain and adopt Janeway's combination of formality and intimacy with his own crew.

"Well, ladies and gentlemen," he said, "I can't imagine a finer crew. Let's get to work, shall we?"

He shared the turbolift ride to the bridge with Kim and Campbell. A year ago, the three of them would have chatted easily on the brief trip. But this time, no one talked. No one was quite sure of his or her role yet, and there was a stiffness, an awkwardness, that Chakotay didn't like and that he hoped would go away soon.

He was very conscious that he was stepping onto a bridge he knew so well as its captain for the first time. He found he had to stop in midstride and deliberately make his way to the captain's chair instead of his "usual" seat to Janeway's left. Once seated in a chair that he had always associated with one of Starfleet's finest, he looked around, taking in all the changes: the dark-haired woman at the conn instead of the fair-haired man, the slender blonde at ops instead of Harry Kim, Kim himself at Tuvok's old station. A first officer sitting beside him instead of a captain. He trailed his fingers along the back of his chair.

Change is the only certainty, he thought.

He settled himself into his chair, aware that everyone was waiting for him, and spoke his first order as captain.

"*Voyager* to McKinley Station operations. Request permission for departure."

"This is station operations. You are cleared to depart, *Voyager.*"

"Clear all moorings."

"All moorings are clear, sir."

"Take us out, Lieutenant Tare. One-quarter impulse power."

"Aye, sir," Tare replied, executing her captain's order. "Ahead one-quarter impulse power."

Chakotay watched as the gray of the space dock gave way to a field of black with glittering stars. As if he were releasing his own moorings, he took a deep breath and felt his chest expand as his lungs filled with air.

Tare spoke again. "We are free and clear to navigate, sir." Free and clear. *Both good words,* Chakotay thought. "Request course heading," Tare continued.

"Course heading one three mark four," he said. "To Deep Space 6."

Soft sounds of small pads being pressed. Then, "Course laid in, Captain."

And then he gave *the* order: "Engage."

The ship surged into warp, and for a while, Chakotay simply sat quietly, watching as the stars streaked by. But that halcyon moment passed quickly, and he suddenly realized that he didn't know what to do. Should he continue to sit in the chair, the new captain in his proper place, and gaze at the screen? Should he walk around the bridge, checking in with his crew? Mysteriously excuse himself to his ready room to work on something in private?

How the hell did Janeway manage it?

He'd know what to do if he were in Ellis's chair. And he'd have known what to do if he were still in the Maquis, captaining his own small ship and crew. But in these first few awkward moments as captain of a Federation starship, especially this one, he wasn't sure of his role.

Chakotay thought of the enormous Black Jaguar, the powerful animal spirit totem who had appeared to him when he had visited his homeworld a few months ago. Black Jaguar was all about power and focus and a clear vision of a just cause. She'd be laughing her furry tail off if she could see him now.

The thought made him smile, and in that moment of humor, he had the clarity he sought.

He wasn't bucking for captain; he *was* the captain. He didn't have to prove anything to anybody. He just needed to trust himself to do the right thing.

He rose and offered his seat to Ellis. "This first mission is all about the colonists," he told his first officer. "Notify Marius Fortier and have him meet me in my quarters."

Fortier had clearly been eager for the meeting, as Chakotay had barely stepped into his own quarters when his door chimed.

Amused, he called, "Enter."

There was a hiss as the door opened. The leader of the colonists was tall and rangy. Despite the fact that he had spent several years on Earth, Marius Fortier still had the bearing of someone who was not overly comfortable in formal society. Nonetheless, he shook Chakotay's outstretched hand firmly.

"It's good to meet you, Mr. Fortier. I suggested we meet here rather than in my ready room because I thought we would be less likely to be disturbed," said Chakotay. "I hope this suits you."

"Wherever you wish, Captain," said Fortier. He had a very slight trace of a French accent. "I am pleased you wished to speak with me at all."

Chakotay wondered what kind of runaround the man had gotten.

"I've nothing else scheduled for the moment, so we can take our time," he said. "I was just about to have some coffee. May I offer you something to drink?"

"Thank you. Vulcan spiced tea, hot," said Fortier.

Chakotay ordered coffee and removed both steaming cups from the replicator.

"Sounds like you've developed some sophisticated tastes while you were waiting to return to Loran II," he said, handing the tea to Fortier. "Vulcan spiced tea doesn't appeal to everyone."

"Our Federation contact was a Vulcan," Fortier explained, inhaling the aroma and then sipping the hot beverage. "She introduced me to it and I grew to enjoy it." He arched an eyebrow and added, "I may enjoy Vulcan spiced tea, Captain, but I would not call myself nor any of my fellow colonists a sophisticate."

He used the word as if it were an insult. Chakotay felt a hint of amusement; for many centuries on Earth, the French were considered to be some of the most sophisticated humans on the planet, but Fortier clearly wanted no part of that aspect of his heritage.

Chakotay indicated they should sit. After another sip of coffee, he decided it was time to quit beating around the bush. Indicating a padd, he said, "Of course I've read everything about Loran II's history, but Starfleet reports tend to be a bit dry. I'd like to hear the whole story from you, if you don't mind."

"Certainly," agreed Fortier. "But before I begin, let me say that I've done my reading about you as well. I am grateful that we are in the hands of someone who personally understands our situation."

Chakotay inclined his head. "Our histories have many similarities, but your situation is unique to you. That's what I'm interested in hearing about."

Fortier's full lips curved in a tentative smile. Chakotay felt himself warming to the man. He seemed so eager for someone to understand him and his people.

"Very well, then. Before the war, we were happily ensconced on Loran II," he began. "The colony was entering its fifteenth year. Many children knew it as their only home. It was a bountiful planet and we had all we needed. We maintained contact with the Federation, of course, and from time to time Starfleet vessels would come to repair damaged equipment or replenish certain supplies."

"How was your relationship with these people?"

"Good enough. We never thought of ourselves as escaping from the Federation and its tenets, merely as expanding them. It was always good to see new faces, and we were happy to provide them with a pleasant place for shore leave." His eyes grew sad. "One hates to romanticize the past, but I must tell you, Captain, I don't exaggerate when I tell you it was an idyllic life."

Chakotay thought back to his recent visit to Dorvan V, when he and his sister Sekaya rediscovered their youth and swam and sunned on rocks. He thought of the feasts, of the celebrations and rituals, of the deeply contented looks on his parents' faces for most of their lives. He had been the contrary, the one who had been driven to look elsewhere for his destiny, but he knew that for most of the people on Dorvan V, their existence had been idyllic too.

"I understand," he said, which was not the same thing as agreeing.

Fortier continued.

"The only trouble we had known came in the form of the Federation-Cardassian treaty of 2370. Our world, like yours, was one of those ceded to the Cardassians as part of the price of keeping the peace. Many of us, myself included, did not want to go back to Earth. We had grown to think of Loran II as our home. Most of us were persuaded to evacuate, but not all. Almost a quarter of the colonist families chose to remain behind. While it more than met our rather simple needs, Loran II is not a particularly rich planet, not in the way the rest of the galaxy reckons richness, and we felt certain that the Cardassians had more important things to think about than our little world."

The colonists on Dorvan V had taken that same gamble. They had trusted that their "little world" held no pressing interest for the Cardassians, and they had been lucky in that their guess had been accurate.

Such had at first seemed to be the case with Loran II as well, Chakotay knew. Since the end of the war until just recently, those who had elected to remain behind had been in fairly regular contact with those who had chosen to evacuate.

"According to my report," said Chakotay, "shortly before you began to move toward resuming residence on Loran II, you lost contact with those colonists who had elected to stay."

Fortier nodded, sighed, and sipped his cooling tea. "True. We have no idea why. It could be anything, from simple equipment damage—that is, of course, our hope—to a swift, devastating illness to an attack."

"Nothing we've heard indicates the latter," Chakotay said quickly.

"Of course, but until we can get there and see for ourselves, we will not know conclusively." His voice trembled ever so slightly. "I left a brother behind, Captain. You must know I am hoping for the best."

"As am I—and everyone in the Federation," Chakotay said earnestly. This was the one of the first real efforts toward regaining normalcy that had happened since the war. It would be good for morale if the only problem was a damaged communication device.

Besides, there was that stubborn Federation trait of wanting all its members to be peaceful, happy, and prosperous.

"Thank you, Captain. Is there anything else you wish to ask of me?"

"Not at the moment, no." Chakotay hesitated, then said, "I trust my first officer took good care of you when you came on board?"

"Yes, but he is very formal."

"He takes this mission seriously," said Chakotay, assuming that this was true.

Fortier's dark eyes flashed. "There is no one on this ship who takes this mission more seriously than I," Fortier said. "But we are casual men and women, Captain. We are a free people. We do not take kindly to being told to stay in our quarters like animals in a pen."

"Of course not," said Chakotay. "I assure you, Commander Ellis was only following proper protocol. This is this ship's first mission with this new crew—and new captain," he added. "You might experience some of our . . . growing pains. Please know that all your people will have the run of the ship once we're under way."

"Thank you," said Fortier, relaxing visibly.

"You may want to visit our counselor," said Chakotay. "We're fortunate in that we were assigned a Huanni. We want you to feel free to express any concerns you might have about returning to Loran II."

"You must understand there are no so-called concerns," Fortier said. "We are going home. We are worried about those who were left behind, but that is all."

Chakotay knew he was pushing. Fortier was clearly an independent man, and he didn't want to risk alienating him further.

"As you see fit, of course. If any of your people do decide to visit her, anything they share with her will remain confidential."

"I understand." Fortier hesitated. "We had another request, Captain. Was it possible for it to be granted?"

"Oh, yes, you asked for a spiritual adviser. We'll be picking one up on Deep Space 6 very soon."

"Ah, good, good."

Chakotay hesitated. "I don't mean to pry, but . . . Astall is a very competent counselor."

"And you are wondering, why do we need another person to talk to? I am certain your Astall is brilliant. But, Captain, I can tell a counselor, 'I am worried about my brother's safety,' and she can help me handle my anxiety. But if I say, 'I am worried about my brother's soul,' what is she to say to that?"

The man had an excellent point. "My father would have liked you and your people very much."

Fortier smiled a little. "I hope his son does too. Is that all, Captain?"

"I think so, for now." Both men rose and shook hands. The door hissed as Fortier exited. Chakotay exhaled. He had a completely fresh appreciation for his friend Kathryn Janeway. But he had a certain problem that she hadn't had—Priggy for a first officer.

It was time they had The Talk.

Chapter
4

TORCHLIGHT FLICKERED on the steam rising from the fissures in the stone, illuminating it as it curled upward to caress rapt faces with its sinuous tendrils. The lava below bathed everything in a red, eerie glow. The heat scoured, purified; it burned away everything that was not clean, not focused, not its raw, true self. The low drone of chanting created a rhythm that hummed along the very bones, throbbed with each heartbeat, a rhythm that both soothed and inspired. The assembled figures clustered together, opened mind and body to the steam and the heat and the visions that would come, staring at the pulsing molten rock.

Lieutenant Commander Tom Paris wanted to wipe at the sweat that greased his brow before it dripped into his eyes, but knew better than to make the gesture. It would be a sign of discomfort, and discomfort was viewed as weakness. His nasal passages burned from the steam, and the heavy Klingon clothing he was forced to wear was unbearably hot. He swallowed, a difficult trick to perform with a thick, parched tongue. He thought he might pass out from the heat and lack of water. While normally fainting, too, would be a sign of weakness, here it would shout to the assembled Klingons that the human Tom Paris had been chosen for a vision.

Well, he thought, *a man can hope.*

He had actually thought he might eventually get used to all this, physically if not emotionally, but he'd had no such luck. Even B'Elanna, half-human as she was, had a tougher time with it than the other Klingons who had come on pilgrimage to the sacred planet of Boreth in search of visions of Kahless.

Paris had always felt that B'Elanna needed to better integrate her Klingon self with her human self, but he worried about the toll this particular form of integration was taking on her. Still, when they had finished their required prayer sessions and meetings and meditations, and they were alone in their quarters with their incredibly gorgeous six-month-old daughter Miral, there was an aura of peace surrounding his wife that touched his heart.

He just hoped that she would get what she needed from Boreth sooner rather than later.

Paris found he missed being on a ship. More to the

point, he missed his friends and having something useful to do with his time. He was well aware that he was here under special dispensation until such time as Starfleet needed him or B'Elanna chose to leave. And it wasn't that he was ungrateful for the privilege. For a while there, Tom respected Klingon tradition more than his wife did. But he didn't want to be on Boreth as "B'Elanna Torres's husband" any more than she would want to be on a ship only as "Tom Paris's wife."

When the sound of a massive gong shuddered along Paris's bones, it was all he could do not to shout, "Hooray!" Unsteadily he got to his feet and helped B'Elanna to hers. It was time for the next round of supplicants to enter the lava caves and experience heat- and chemical-induced delusions. He wished them many happy visions.

They said no word as they made their way from the lava pits up the winding stairs to the room that served as Boreth's nursery. They were not the only parents who felt the call to go on pilgrimage, and Tom was surprised and pleased to discover that the Klingons had no problems accommodating young children. There were eight of them in residence now. Most of the children were old enough to amuse themselves, but there were a few who were still very young and needed looking after. At six months, Miral was the youngest "pilgrim."

Tom had to smother a smile as he nodded to Kularg, the gruff, grizzled warrior who minded the children. The Klingons so often surprised him. Just when you thought you had them stereotyped as proud, honorable, sometimes overly zealous warriors, they'd play the "family is important" card and make babysitting nearly as honorable as beheading someone who insulted you.

Tom and B'Elanna bowed slightly. Kularg accepted the honor with fierce eyes.

"I honor you for your commitment to the future generations," B'Elanna said formally.

"The honor is mine, to shape the future," Kularg replied in his deep rumble.

They gathered up their daughter and went to their quarters. The minute the heavy wooden door was closed behind them Tom expelled a great breath.

"By Kahless's beard," he said, inventing an oath, "I'm thirsty. You?"

He poured mugs of water for them both. B'Elanna grabbed hers and gulped down half of it in answer. He drank his own greedily and poured himself a second mug. Try as he might to wash them clean, the cups always seemed to have the faintest hint of bloodwine about them. Probably because if any proper Klingon saw them drinking water instead of that popular beverage they'd insult their parents.

My dad can take whatever insult a Klingon can dish out, he thought. *I'm drinking the damn water.*

Their room, like much of the monastery, was comparatively new. It had been painstakingly reconstructed after the monastery had been razed in the coup attempt against Martok. B'Elanna had told him that while everything belowground had escaped relatively undamaged—including an apparently impressive library—the ancient monastery had been leveled. Tom was surprised that so much had been achieved in such a short time. Some parts of the monastery were still under construction, but much had already been restored. Even more astonishing, the building had been done by hand, as it would have been done in the ancient days. Artisans and architects from throughout the Empire had been summoned to rebuild this sacred place stone by stone. Many who had ancient artifacts in private collections donated the priceless pieces. Tom had wondered why— surely, it would have been faster and easier to just replicate what was needed. But according to the rather imposing Commander Logt, one of Emperor Kahless's personal guards and the only one stationed here on Boreth, the gifts were to honor the spirits of those who had first constructed the monasteries.

The only light was provided by candles, torches, fires, and, of course, the lava pits themselves. Rooms were sparsely furnished, and only with the rudest of chairs, benches and tables. There were no beds, only mats on the floor covered with animal hides. Bathing was limited to whatever one could manage with a basin of water. Meals were served twice a day and consisted entirely of traditional Klingon food. Tom had actually learned to like *gagh*, and to his eternal surprise, found that he agreed with the Klingon assertion that the worms were, indeed, best when eaten live.

B'Elanna handed Miral to him, who wriggled and kicked in his arms. Whatever annoyance and resentment Tom felt at being on Boreth always melted whenever he held his daughter. He knew he was fortunate to be able to spend so much time with her. He smiled down at the infant.

"Who's a good little *Kuvah'Magh* then?" he cooed, bouncing her a little. She blew a spit bubble. He thought it adorable and amazingly clever.

B'Elanna had shrugged out of her tunic and now reached for the baby, bringing the hungry infant to her breast. She settled down on the thick animal skin on the stone floor. Tom felt deeply content as he watched them.

"Madonna and child," he said.

She glowered at him, utterly destroying the image. "You keep bringing that up."

"Well," he said, changing out of his own sweat-encrusted clothes into something resembling clean ones, "and why not? It was really meeting Kohlar and his ship of the faithful that rekindled your interest in your Klingon heritage. And that led us here."

She sighed. "I suppose you're right."

He sat down beside her on the skin that served as their bed and stroked her bare shoulder. What he didn't say was that encountering the Klingons who believed that their child was a savior had changed him as well. Tom knew that B'Elanna pooh-poohed the whole thing, but he wasn't so sure.

"Have you thought about my suggestion?" he ventured carefully.

"Clubbing Kularg, snatching Miral, and . . . what was your phrase, 'blowing this joint'?"

Tom laughed and kissed her shoulder. "No, the other, less potentially painful suggestion."

"Yes, I've thought about it. I don't know, Tom. It might not be less potentially painful in the long run."

"They really need to know, hon," he said, more seriously. "I know the Doc shared all his medical knowledge with Starfleet and the Empire, but the Klingons really ought to know the whole *Kuvah'Magh* story."

"The Empire knows."

"They know a dry, impersonal log. They don't know how closely Miral fits the prophecies. And besides, you can't tell me you aren't just a little bit curious to see what else is out there that talks about our daughter."

"Coincidences happen all the time, Tom," Torres said, exasperation creeping into her voice. "It's only in stories that they mean anything."

"Still, it's a nice chunk of Klingon history, and whether or not she is the Savior, I would like to know if there are any other scrolls about her."

"About her? Who, Miral or the Savior?"

He ducked the question in a rather devilish fashion. He got behind her on the bed and began massaging her neck. She closed her eyes and said softly, "Mmmmm . . . that feels good."

"And that?"

"Mmm . . . yes, right there."

"And . . . *that*. . . ."

"Very . . . um . . . very nice. . . ."

"Talk to them tomorrow about getting permission to visit the scroll room?"

"You cunning little . . . oh. Oh. *Come here.*"

Libby Webber, renowned musician and Starfleet Intelligence operative, had decided that she was not going to cry when she said good-bye to Harry Kim.

She had had brave words for Captain Chakotay about the mission, and in her good moments she believed them. But she remembered kissing Harry good-bye nearly eight years before, when he had left to go to Deep Space 9 and join *Voyager* as the wet-behind-the-ears ops officer. He was different, and she was very different—more than she could let him know—but there were eerie similarities between the two farewells despite her laughter and feigned nonchalance.

So she was very pleased with herself when she didn't cry, not even when he kissed her tenderly and said, "See you in a few weeks." And then, further challenging her determination to shed no tears, "I don't suppose you've changed your mind?"

A month ago, he had proposed. She had been stunned and stammered out a refusal her heart hadn't wanted to make. She couldn't tell him about her real day job, and she wasn't prepared to try to make a life with someone she had to lie to. At least, not yet. She wasn't sure she'd ever be ready. So she had had to watch his open, honest face fall. The last few weeks had been strained. She hoped that time apart would help them both accept the way things had to be for now.

She transported back to her cabin in Maine feeling heavy and unhappy, and realizing that she had several messages waiting for her didn't cheer her up in the slightest. She ignored them for a few moments while she cuddled on the floor with Binky, her rabbit, then sighed and, like Harry, went on duty.

"How did the launch go?" asked her boss, Director of Covert Operations Aidan Fletcher. Both of them had snagged promotions six months ago after they had assisted in stopping Fletcher's predecessor from succeeding in a brutal and clever plot against Earth and the Federation itself. Despite the fact that before Harry had returned, Libby and the elegant, slender Aidan had been romantically involved, Libby was now comfortable working for him again. Aidan knew how she felt about Harry, and in fact he himself had been the one to end his relationship with Libby. Now Aidan was on a very short list of people she completely trusted.

"Without a hitch," she said.

"Good. Any likely suspects?"

The last time the director of covert operations had instructed Libby to search for a mole in the Federation, it had been to throw the young agent off the scent of what was really happening in covert ops. Now, though,

Libby and Fletcher were on the trail of the real thing. There was someone embedded in the Federation who was accessing classified information for purposes unknown. Libby and several other agents, whose names she did not know for security reasons, were trying to hunt the culprit down.

Libby shrugged. "It was difficult to really engage anyone in conversation," she said, wincing inwardly at her Freudian choice of the word "engage." "The focus was really on Chakotay and the party."

"And of course, since he's about to leave for several weeks, I suspect our Lieutenant Kim probably wasn't too keen on your mixing and mingling," said Fletcher wryly, his gray eyes twinkling.

"Well, there is that," she admitted.

"Not to worry. Now that Harry's off on a dull-as-dishwater mission, you've got some time to follow up on these names."

He pressed a button and a list of names sprang up on her console. Her jaw dropped slightly as the list scrolled on and on, and Aidan laughed.

"I know, it's a lot," he said, "but I have the utmost faith in you, Agent Webber."

"Thank you *so* much," she replied, her voice dripping with sarcasm. "You do know I have a concert to prepare for? Several, in fact?"

"And you'll notice that I have thoughtfully given you a list of names of people who are scheduled to appear at said concerts," he said. "No, no need to thank me. Just do your usual excellent job and we'll nail this mole."

He winked and logged off. Libby shook her head. She looked at the list of names once more, sighed, and retrieved her *lal-shak*. She wanted to spend a few moments with its soothing music before tackling a list like that.

Paraphrasing Gilbert and Sullivan, she played and hummed, "A secret agent's lot is not a happy one, happy one."

Chapter
5

THE GROUND TREMBLED as if it were in pain.

Gradak's eyes snapped open as his bed shuddered. He briefly wondered if it was an earthquake. Months of running and hiding had taught him how to awaken fully in an instant, and he was out of bed and on his feet when the second blast came. It knocked him to the floor.

No earthquake, this. This was something different, something more dangerous.

This was phaser fire.

Gradak always slept in his clothes, another habit born of necessity, and now he seized his weapons and his communicator. The minute he tapped the device, though, he realized that the enemy had put up a dampening field.

"Bastards!" he cried. Apparently it wasn't enough to launch what was, by the sound of it, a full-scale attack on a moon that was host to hundreds of families. They had to make sure no one could coordinate escape efforts as well. Still cursing, Gradak raced outside into a nightmare of flame and terror.

The night sky was lit up with fire. Even as he ran out of his home it was struck by screaming phaser blasts and burst into flames. Shrieks of terror assaulted his ears, and by the glow of the orange, crackling flames he saw figures racing to and fro. Some were running with purpose, as he was; others were just fleeing in panic.

I told them we needed to drill for this! Gradak thought in anguish. But the three thousand who called this base home wanted to believe it would never be discovered. Wanted to believe they could leave the danger, the risk, the death out there, out in space. Gradak desperately wished they had listened to his warnings, but by their very nature the Maquis were idealists. And this time, their idealism was going to cost them everything.

There were several dozen small vessels on Tevlik's moon, all designed for speed and maneuverability as well as attack. On an ordinary base, they would be clustered together. Everyone would know where to go. But here, they were scattered; they made more difficult targets that way, but they also made it harder for anyone to escape.

More phaser fire. More screaming. The air grew thick with smoke, and Gradak choked on the stomach-

turning stench of burning flesh. There were people he loved on this Maquis base. But because of the Jem'Hadar dampening field—it had to be the Cardassians and their new-found allies; the Federation would arrest them and confiscate their ships, but they would never authorize this kind of massacre—Gradak could not contact any of those he loved. He could only hope they knew where to find his ship and would meet him there.

The Cardassians continued their attack. Gradak watched, sickened, as a long sheet of deadly phaser fire sliced across the soil. There were sounds of explosions; the blasts had struck ships. But the dreadful sounds came from the west, and Gradak's little ship was to the north.

Tears stung his eyes—a physical reaction to the smoke, an emotional reaction to the horror that greeted him everywhere he looked. He blinked hard, refusing to acknowledge the pathetic cries for help, refusing to stop to offer assistance, feeling a dreadful ache as he did so. Anyone who wasn't on a ship within the next few minutes would be either dead or, if lucky, captured. His only hope to save himself and however many souls he could cram onto his small vessel would be to reach Vallia's Revenge *as soon as possible.*

Before it was destroyed. Before everything was destroyed.

How had this happened? How had the Cardassians discovered the base? It had been operating since the very beginning of the resistance movement, safe and undiscovered. It was the one sanctuary, the one refuge, that no Maquis would reveal. Not even under torture. It was one thing to gasp out military plans and strategies and locations of weapons while being "interrogated" by the Cardassians, but to breathe a word of this place, with the children and the families at risk, to expose it to attack—no Maquis would have done that.

How, then, had this horrific night come to be?

Jarem Kaz bolted upright, gasping for breath.

"Lights," he called in a raspy voice as he fumbled for a glass of water. He gulped the liquid quickly, but it eased his dry mouth only slightly.

He looked around at his pleasant, spacious quarters aboard *Voyager* as his heart slowed to a more normal pace. He wasn't happy that the dream had returned, but he wasn't altogether surprised. For the first time since he had been joined with the Kaz symbiont, Jarem was heading back into an area of space that had figured in the war. The colonists on board weren't Maquis, of course, but Loran II was located in space that had formerly belonged to the Cardassians. It was only natural that Kaz's subconscious, here on his first official day as a member of this ship's crew, might seize upon the worst memory of a previous host and gnaw on it.

His heart and breathing slowed as he sipped the water. The further away he moved from the dream, the less concerned he was. It was a natural reaction. And one bad dream wasn't worth worrying about.

He called for the lights again, settled back onto his bed, and waited for sleep for a second time that night.

The next morning, Chakotay asked Commander Ellis to join him for a private chat. While Marius Fortier might have felt more comfortable being received in Chakotay's quarters, *Voyager*'s captain knew that Ellis would deem the ready room much more appropriate.

Deciding to break the ice quickly, Chakotay handed Ellis a padd the moment the door closed behind him.

"What's this, sir?" asked Ellis.

"The duty roster," Chakotay said. "I used to hate drawing these up. It's one thing I won't mind handing over to you, Andrew. Or do you prefer Andy, or perhaps Drew?"

Chakotay suspected he preferred Commander Ellis, but the younger man replied somewhat stiffly, "Andrew will be fine, sir. In informal situations, of course."

Chakotay smiled. "Of course," he agreed. "Have a seat."

Ellis glanced uncomfortably back at the closed door that opened onto the bridge.

"Lieutenant Kim's on duty, and believe me, he knows enough to holler for help if he needs it. Have a seat," Chakotay repeated, a little more insistently.

Ellis obeyed, perching on the edge of the sofa. If it was possible for anyone to look like he was standing at attention while sitting, Ellis could.

"You and I haven't had much chance to talk," Chakotay began. "I'd like to rectify that."

"Captain Chakotay," said Ellis, his discomfort palpable, "I enjoy relaxing with friends as much as anyone on this ship." Somehow, Chakotay didn't believe that. "But I hardly think that while we are both on duty is an appropriate time for such activities."

"And you'd be right," Chakotay said. "We'll be dining together tonight for that." Ellis looked startled but resigned at the news. Chakotay had decided that for the time being, he needed to make "relaxing with friends" an order or Ellis would find some reason to object to it. It wasn't easy for a rising young Starfleet officer to get comments like "works too hard" on his reviews—hard work was expected and usually admired and encouraged—but somehow, Andrew Ellis had managed it.

"What I wanted to tell you," Chakotay continued, "is that while I respect your way of going about your job, it's a job that I myself have held for quite some time. I know what it takes. I'll give you a lot of freedom, Andrew, but I'll be watching you."

Ellis clearly misunderstood Chakotay's words and bridled slightly.

"Captain, with all due respect, I have received nothing but praise for how I have gone about my duties in the past. If you are suggesting that I would neglect—"

"Quite the opposite," Chakotay assured him. "I'll be watching to you make sure you don't exhaust yourself."

"I hardly think—"

Chakotay set his cup on the table. "Let's speak frankly. I know you wanted this assignment. I know your record. I know how highly thought of you are in Starfleet, and how capable you are. You know that you weren't my first choice for first officer, and we both know that you've acquired the nickname 'Priggy.' "

Ellis's pale blue eyes widened slightly and his face colored. *Uh oh,* Chakotay thought. *Maybe he* didn't *know that.*

Barreling on, he continued, "We also both know how those of us who spent the last years in the Delta Quadrant are thought of among certain segments of the population, especially in Starfleet. I can't tell you how often someone has called us 'lucky.' I don't think the families of those who died trying to get *Voyager* home believe their loved ones were lucky. I've read the reports, I've talked to the survivors, I have some grasp of what the Alpha Quadrant has undergone while we were dealing with our own difficulties. It's been harder for us to reintegrate ourselves into society than you might think. There's a mixture on board now of former *Voyager* crew and Dominion War veterans, and that's reflected in the ship's captain and its first officer."

He couldn't read Ellis's expression, but now that he had opened the proverbial can of worms, Chakotay continued.

"The people I've served with over the last seven years are fully capable of focusing their attention and making split-second decisions. We'd never have made it back if that wasn't the case. But they may be a little more relaxed than you're used to, a little more casual, and perhaps even a bit irreverent. Don't make the mistake of assuming that a laid-back attitude in the mess hall or on the holodeck indicates incompetence."

"Captain, I believe that making such an assumption would indeed be a mistake," Ellis said rather pointedly. Chakotay noticed with pleasure that Ellis now looked more amused than offended. Good.

Ellis said, "You do realize that one of the reasons I was assigned as your first officer was to temper your, um, irreverence?"

"I do," Chakotay said, "but I outrank you."

Ellis paused before speaking, trying to gather his thoughts.

"Permission to speak freely?" he said at last.

"By all means."

"I don't know if this leopard can change his spots," Ellis said, "or, frankly, if he even wants to. But I understand your meaning, Captain. I respect what those who served aboard *Voyager* went through. And though you may not believe it, I respect the former Maquis among this crew as well. They put up a good fight long before the rest of the Federation got on board. And once reinstated, they continued to fight well. I'm sure you know by now that those who are left are highly regarded these days."

Those who are left. Chakotay remembered receiving

65

the letter from Sveta, the horrible missive that told him that an overwhelming majority of the Maquis had been killed. It had felt like a punch in the gut when he read those words, and had affected him deeply. It had affected every former Maquis on *Voyager,* perhaps especially B'Elanna, who had resorted to increasingly risky holodeck programs in order that she might feel something, anything. He couldn't believe it when he stepped onto the holodeck and into a program she'd designed that showcased murdered, bloody Maquis bodies in a labyrinthine cave system, complete with grinning, maniacal Cardassians for her to fight.

His mind went back to a time even before then, before he and his crew had been snatched by the Caretaker. He saw Arak Katal's friendly Bajoran face, a pleasant mask that had hidden an evil Chakotay couldn't even begin to grasp. He wondered again, as he had a thousand times before, what possibly could have driven a Bajoran to betray his own people in such a brutal fashion.

"Captain?" Ellis's voice jolted him back to the present. To cover his woolgathering, Chakotay smiled reassuringly at his new first officer.

"We're creating something new here, a fresh start," Chakotay said. "Let's you and I set the example." He extended his hand.

Without hesitation, Ellis grasped it firmly. "I'd be honored, sir."

* * *

One thing that was SOP early on in a ship's first few missions was that everyone needed to have a routine physical. It was not a top priority, but since the trip to Loran II promised to be uneventful, Chakotay had issued the order and assumed that Kaz would see a goodly number of people showing up who were simply looking for something to do.

Chakotay also decided he'd be the one to set the example. When he arrived in sickbay, he was not surprised to see three crew members getting this particular duty out of the way early. He had not met any of them yet and hoped he could use this opportunity to introduce himself and chat a bit. They were all lying on beds, and as one they bolted upright and would have slipped to the floor to stand as he entered. He waved them back.

"As you were," he said, trying and failing to stifle a grin. Hesitantly they obeyed, but he could tell his presence here was rattling them. They were all fresh out of the Academy and seemed very nervous. As he looked at the three sets of wide, admiring eyes, he thought, *They're so young they didn't fight in the Dominion War, and the adventure of* Voyager *is probably quite appealing.*

After a few awkward moments spent futilely trying to engage them in pleasant chitchat, Chakotay retreated to Kaz's office, trying to keep out of the way until the doctor had finished with the three recent cadets. When they left, all of them casting furtive, awestruck glances behind them at their captain, Chakotay hopped onto a bed.

"Looks like you're the only one on the ship who's got his hands full," Chakotay commented.

"This is a first," said Kaz, glancing down at his medical tricorder as he scanned Chakotay. "I've served on a ship before, and I always practically had to beg the crew to come in for their baseline physicals."

"It's been a pretty quiet trip so far," said Chakotay.

Kaz's blue eyes flickered to Chakotay's brown ones. "And that's a problem?"

"No," Chakotay replied. "Just unusual. It was hard to be bored in the Delta Quadrant."

"I can imagine," said Kaz. "Borg, Hirogen, Kazon . . . you had your hands full. Now, lie down and let the good doctor put some cortical monitors on."

Chakotay obeyed. There was a comfortable silence between the friends, punctuated only by the occasional sound of the equipment as it hummed and beeped.

Finally, Chakotay said, "Jarem . . . I wanted to ask you a question."

"Go ahead."

"Has this mission been stirring up any . . . any memories for you?"

Kaz again looked at him piercingly. "Yes, as a matter of fact, it has. This is the first time I've been directly involved in anything that has to do with the Cardassians, even peripherally, since Gradak's death. Since I received the Kaz symbiont."

"Same for me," said Chakotay. "I was talking to Ellis and he brought up the fact that there are so few

Maquis left. I couldn't help but think about Arak Katal."

"Bastard," Kaz said as calmly as if he were ordering tea from the replicator. "I tell you, Chakotay, I truly hope we find him one day. It would be immensely satisfying to testify at his trial. That's the best I could hope for since the Federation frowns on executions."

Chakotay coughed quietly, but Kaz too had heard the sound of the doors hissing open. Two more fresh-faced youngsters stood there, practically gaping at beholding the Great Captain Chakotay.

"All right, Captain," Kaz said, "I've completed the physical. You may go."

Chakotay smiled at the newcomers, who gazed back at him with round eyes. He was all in favor of a crew respecting their captain—hell, no one had respected Janeway more than he—but this attitude was ridiculous.

Time to start getting to know his crew.

Chapter

6

JANEWAY POURED HERSELF another cup of coffee and settled back down at her desk at Starfleet Headquarters. She sipped the aromatic beverage—even after six months of drinking the real stuff again, she delighted in it—and looked at her "to do" list.

She knew that all of her former crew had had an . . . interesting time trying to adjust to "regular" life here in the Alpha Quadrant after seven years of journeying, but she wondered if anyone—with the exceptions of Icheb and Seven of Nine—had had to make a more convoluted leap than she. It was quite a change, going from captain of a lost starship to a desk job here at Starfleet Headquarters. She had always thought that if such a situation ever came to pass, she'd feel like a bird with clipped wings, but to her surprise Janeway wasn't sure she wasn't enjoying it.

Janeway was a natural teacher, and she loved every minute of the class she and Tuvok were teaching. The young minds seated behind the desks were like sponges, soaking up everything she said. It didn't hurt that the two old friends were teaching a fascinating subject—the Borg. Just yesterday the students had been treated to a question-and-answer session with Icheb and Seven, who had graciously volunteered to subject themselves to scrutiny. It had been a marvelous class. Janeway thought that more had been done in those two hours to dispel prejudice against Borg victims than had been done in the last fifteen years, and she was very proud of both of her former honorary crew members.

In fact, she had a few moments before her next scheduled appointment. Glancing at the chronometer, she realized that the think tank would be on its break. One of its members, a Mnari, had to sleep every three hours for at least ten minutes at a stretch or its powerful brain would suffer damage. It also, according to Seven, had to eat every two hours, so there was a constant supply of food available to what the Doctor had taken to calling the "Tankers." "Hence," he had lamented, "the ready availability of ammunition for the recent food fight."

"Computer, contact Seven of Nine."

Seven's lovely face appeared on the viewscreen. She smiled. "Admiral. How nice to see you. How may I be of assistance?"

"Just checking in to see how you were doing after your inquisition yesterday."

Seven arched a brow. "It was hardly an inquisition. Your students were perspicacious and attentive. It was a pleasure imparting information to them."

"Still, they went at you pretty intensely. I was hoping that you didn't have any negative reactions afterward."

"Admiral Janeway," said Seven bluntly, "I have endured more severe interrogation at the hands of Starfleet officials. I regenerated without incident."

"Good. How are things going? You and I didn't get much of a chance to talk yesterday."

"Quite well, except," she looked around and said softly, "I am concerned about the Doctor."

"Really? Why?"

"He is putting a great deal of hope into his presentation. Too much, I think. He will be speaking to a group of individuals who are entrenched in their own opinions, and his speech, no matter how eloquent or logical, is unlikely to sway them."

Janeway felt a stab of sympathy. Oliver Baines, though a champion of holographic rights, had really been no friend to holograms; he had done more harm than good. No one was feeling particularly sympathetic toward the issue now. It was a bad time for the Doctor to be speaking.

"Well, he's a big hologram, he can take whatever they dish out." She smiled at Seven. "You've got a good heart, Seven."

"The heart is not the seat of emotions as poets would have us believe, Admiral. It is merely an organ whose sole function is to circulate blood throughout the body. Any kindness or sympathy I feel for the Doctor originates in the brain, particularly in the—"

"Now you're teasing me, Seven."

She smiled. "Yes, I confess I am."

How far she's come, Janeway thought. "Regardless of where the emotions originate, I'm glad you're there to support him."

"As am I."

A shrill *whoot-whoot-whoot* sound made both women wince. "Ah," said Seven, "Jish is awake. I need to return to duty, Admiral. Was there anything else?"

"Not a thing. Just a hello. Take care of yourself, Seven."

"I will, Admiral. Seven out."

Janeway sat back in her chair and stretched, gathering strength for the next conversation. She thought it would not go quite so well.

While molding young minds was definitely an important task, so was the one that lay before Janeway today—convincing a planet to stay in the Federation. She closed the door to her office, glanced at the chronometer, and said, "Computer, put me through to Amar Kol."

After a second, Amar Merin Kol's pleasant face appeared on the screen. The Kerovians were humanoid, with pale orange skin and red hair, four fingers on each hand, and wide mouths. They had been part of the Federation for nearly forty years. While they did not contribute anything in the way of martial assistance—no Kerovian had yet even expressed an interest in attending the Academy—they were a people who had added greatly to the Federation's accumulated knowledge and had a keen interest in the arts. Janeway knew it would be a loss to the Federation on more than one level, should Kerovi opt to withdraw.

Janeway smiled, and Kol smiled in return. Janeway, at least, had enjoyed talking with the female leader of the planet, and it seemed as though Kol had enjoyed interacting with her as well. If only they were discussing Kerovian symphonies and theater instead of secession.

"Good evening, Admiral Janeway," said Kol in her soft, deep voice. "Or, perhaps, it should be 'good morning' in San Francisco?"

"Bright and early," Janeway replied. "I'm sorry to keep you up so late."

"Not at all," Kol said. "It's always a pleasure to talk to you."

With a twinge of regret, Janeway suspected this was quite true. It was a sentiment she shared.

"Likewise, Amar Kol," she replied sincerely. Kol had always used Janeway's title, so Janeway was careful to use hers. "Have you had a chance to review the statistics I sent a few days ago?"

Kol nodded. "They are very impressive, and I am delighted to hear that so much healing has already been accomplished." She stretched her wide mouth in a sad smile as she continued, "But both you and I know that statistics can be interpreted to say whatever one wants them to say."

Soft, but stubborn. That was Merin Kol, the proverbial iron fist in a velvet glove. The leader of the Kerovians was slender, with delicate features, and she always wore flowing, fine garments. Janeway had to wonder if the choice was deliberate, if Kol was well aware of how soft a demeanor she presented while remaining strong and resolute. It would be easy to underestimate Kol if one didn't know her well. Inwardly, Janeway sighed.

"Kerovi has always stood firm on its policy of nonviolence," Janeway said, "and the Federation has always respected that. You know well that we have never forced your people to contribute troops, not even at the darkest times of the war."

"No, you have not," Kol agreed, "but one does not have to use force in order to exert pressure."

Janeway thought about the statistics she had been reading lately: how many millions had died. Kerovi had a population of two billion, and they had not sent a single person to fight. They had not contributed weapons or vessels or even supplies for the war. The one thing they had done was contribute assistance when it came to helping the victims of the war, willingly providing food, medicines, clothing, and shelter, and for that the Federation was grateful. Still, Janeway couldn't help but feel a twinge of anger.

She resisted the temptation to rise to the subtle bait and continued, "Be that as it may, it still stands that Kerovi didn't suffer a single casualty in the war, and yet it and its people were protected by the Federation."

Kol's gaze was steady. "Protected from attack in a war we did not want," she said. "Kerovi's government—and I personally, Admiral—wanted no part of the Dominion War. We spoke against it. We would not have required such protection from the Federation had not the Federation turned every single planet that belonged to it into a potential target for its enemies."

Her voice was growing harsher, and Janeway changed the subject.

"We've discussed this before, Amar. And we've agreed to disagree. It's a moot point. The fact remains, we won this war, and the planets in the Federation are safe because of that fact."

Kol arched a red eyebrow.

"If there were to be trouble again," Janeway continued, pressing her point, "from a neighbor or another direction, Kerovi would be able to call upon the Federation for assistance. If you secede from it, you would be left completely vulnerable. Your planet has no real way of defending itself."

"Until we joined the Federation, for several thousand years, Kerovi had no need to defend itself. To us, it's cause and effect. Join the Federation, and your planet subsequently requires protection."

"Join the Federation," Janeway said, keeping her

voice calm and even, "and your planet has access to medical and scientific advances as they are discovered and proved safe. Your planet has food if there is a shortfall, technologies to help your people prosper. You're able to participate in shaping the future of the quadrant."

"Admiral," said Kol in a voice of aching sincerity, "I fear for the future of this quadrant, if the last few years have been any indication of where it's going."

She threw up her slender, four-fingered hands in exasperation. "All the things you say are true, but what you're not saying is that the Federation doesn't have a stranglehold on free trade—at least," she amended, "not yet."

Janeway's eyes narrowed. It took effort, but she held her tongue.

"We can obtain food and technologies and medicine through other means. Means that don't force us to ally with a huge, anonymous collection of planets. Means that don't put Kerovi at risk."

Janeway smiled sadly, the anger bleeding out of her. "Why do I feel dizzy?"

Kol smiled too, her pretty face softening. "As if you've been running around in circles? How odd, for I feel the same way."

Janeway hesitated. "You've put forth some passionate arguments, Amar Kol. But you still haven't committed to formally withdrawing. I take it that you will be at the conference?"

Kol nodded. "Yes, I will. I look forward to meeting you in person, Admiral. I think there are many things we would agree about."

"I think so, too. I had best let you get some sleep, Amar."

Kol made a wry face. "Sleep is in short supply for an amar," she said.

"And for admirals," Janeway replied. "Good night, Amar."

When Janeway's face disappeared from the screen, Kol sighed. This was so difficult. Janeway was such a commanding, persuasive presence it was hard to say no to her, even when Kol knew it was the right thing—and the thing both her people and her government wanted.

She rubbed her cheeks, massaging the sensitive cluster of nerves there. It helped her relax.

Amar Merin Kol had come into power by accident six years ago. Her husband had been killed in an accident and she had stepped up out of a sense of duty to serve out his term. She was not prepared to be reelected, and while she strove to uphold her honorable position by studying, learning, and listening, she was glad that she had so many wise people around her to advise her.

Her computer chimed softly, and she realized it was one of those self-same wise people. Smiling, she touched the screen and the familiar face of her friend and adviser, Sul Alamys, appeared.

"Good evening, Amar," Alamys said. "I trust I am not disturbing you?"

"Of course not," Kol said. "My best adviser could never be a disturbance. How has your trip been progressing? What have you learned?"

"A great deal," said Alamys solemnly, "all of which supports our position. Amar, as I predicted, we are not alone in resenting the bullying of the Federation. Of the six representatives I've talked with, three are also considering secession."

"Really?"

The number was startling. Kol had not realized that so many others were discontented. It would seem, she thought sadly, that the Dominion War continued to produce casualties.

Alamys nodded. "There is a disproportionate number of certain species in the Federation, and they are the ones who seem to control it. Humans, Vulcans, Trill, Bolians, and a handful of others compared to the hundreds of species that are represented. We have only a few officials to represent our interests. We are helpless to control what the Federation does, yet must go along with it."

Kol nodded sadly. "Forty years is a long time," she said. "It will be difficult to withdraw."

"And had things continued as they were for the last forty years," Alamys said, "I would not advise withdrawing. But the Federation's policy is tantamount to meddling now, and that meddling led to many deaths.

They don't have to be Kerovian deaths for Kerovi to mourn their loss."

"No, of course not," agreed Kol. "If only the Federation had been more isolationist. Certainly there are enough challenges among its member planets that it didn't need to go to war and create more."

"And that," said Alamys, "is the position of nearly all the planets who are considering withdrawal."

Kol nodded and sighed. "Continue your conversations with these people, Alamys, and keep me apprised," she said. "I will take your observations with me to the conference."

And, she thought sadly, *be the bearer of bad news to Admiral Janeway in person.*

Chapter
7

ENSIGN DAVID CHITTENDEN SETTLED down in *Voyager*'s mess hall with his lunch. Everyone's assignment was new, of course, as this was the ship's first mission since its return to the Alpha Quadrant. But this was Chittenden's first assignment on a starship, and he was more than a bit nervous.

He took a bite of his ham sandwich and chewed thoughtfully, his blue eyes darting around to see who else was present. He decided to play a game with himself, to see if he could tell who was one of the original *Voyagers* and who, like him, was an Alpha Quadrant veteran.

Some of them he knew by sight—Lieutenant Harry

Kim, and of course Lieutenant Vorik, who was his superior officer. Their connection with the ship was well-known. But that cute young woman over there, with the short red hair and the freckles on her nose—she had to be AQV, right out of the Academy. She was too young to have served for seven years. And the fellow over there, tall and rangy, about his own age—he kept glancing around as if he didn't feel comfortable here.

"This seat taken?" came a pleasant female voice.

Chittenden was so startled he spilled his coffee. "Sorry, I didn't hear you. Please, sit down," he said. Blushing, he leaped up to wipe a puddle of coffee off the seat he had just indicated.

"Thanks." The young woman smiled at him as she sat down. When he'd finished cleaning up the spill, she stuck out her hand.

"I'm Lyssa Campbell," she said.

He shook the proffered hand, recognizing the name as that of the ship's ops officer.

"David Chittenden," he said, a little in awe.

"Oh, you're the whiz kid everyone's talking about," she said in a pleased tone of voice, lifting a slice of pizza to her lips.

David felt himself blushing. "Whiz kid?" He sat up a little straighter.

Campbell nodded, chewing on her pizza. She wiped her mouth with her napkin.

"Oh, you bet," she said. "Vorik's mentioned your name to me at least twice. And believe me, from him, that's a real compliment. Welcome aboard *Voyager.*"

"Thanks," he murmured, returning his attention to his sandwich. A long pause ensued. Chittenden tried desperately to think of a topic of conversation.

"Um . . . how does it feel to be back?"

"On *Voyager*?" She considered it. "Good, I think. But a little strange. Seven years is a long time to be with the same crew." She gave him a slow smile. "It's nice to have some new blood."

He was definitely blushing now. "I suppose it would be," he said, rather inanely, he thought. Searching for something to say, he added, "*Voyager*'s a real Starfleet ship now."

The attractive smile faded and the blue eyes were suddenly chilly. David realized he had inserted his foot in his mouth somehow.

"We were a Starfleet ship every minute that we were in the Delta Quadrant," she said, her voice still pleasant but with a hint of warning in it.

Oh, God, Chittenden thought desperately. *Let me say the right thing.*

"Of course you were," he said quickly. "What I meant was, now those who were in the Delta Quadrant can be on the team again."

Her expression grew even colder. David winced inwardly. *Sports metaphors. Bad idea, Dave. Bad idea.*

"We got lost in the Delta Quadrant because Captain Janeway was completing a mission on the orders of Starfleet Command," Campbell said. There was no mistaking her ire now. "Because we were on that mission, we got kidnapped by the Caretaker. Or haven't you read up on your history?"

"Um," said Chittenden.

"We were snatched away from everything we knew and deposited seventy thousand light-years from home. We lost a lot of good people, right at that moment and over the next seven years. But Captain Janeway got us home. A bit of a miracle, if you ask me. And we're here, and we're more than ready to serve. But we were never not on the team, Ensign. Never."

Chittenden replied, "Well, you certainly weren't playing in the Alpha Quadrant. We lost a lot of good people here too, you know. A few *million* good people."

The color rose in her face. She looked even more attractive.

"And how many of those millions of good people did you know and love? I lost friends I'd seen every single day for seven years!"

"I lost friends too, Lieutenant!" Their faces swam into his mind, the pain of their deaths eased only a very little by the ultimate victory over the Dominion. "Friends who willingly boarded ships and headed into battle to fight for the protection of this quadrant, not to just get home and have a nice cup of coffee!"

His eyes widened as the words left his mouth. He couldn't believe what he had just said. This was more than a heated discussion. This could get him slapped down so hard for insubordination—

Campbell stared at him, her blue eyes bright, her face crimson.

"Lieutenant Campbell, I'm—"

She rose, taking her tray. "Excuse me."

David watched her go, mentally kicking himself. He drew a deep breath and for the first time noticed that he was being watched. Some of the faces turned to him were angry or hurt. But other faces—those of the cute young red-haired woman and the rangy fellow, for instance—had slight smiles on them, and he received more than a few subtle nods of approval.

He had completely lost his appetite. Chittenden returned the remains of his uneaten meal to the replicator. Part of him wanted to seek Campbell out and make sure she heard his full apology. But another part of him thought that although his words had certainly been inappropriate, the sentiment wasn't.

Voyager had nothing—*nothing*—on the torment those in the Alpha Quadrant had undergone in its absence. The lives that had been lost on this ship over the last seven years were a drop in the bucket compared to what those who had stayed behind had endured.

No, Chittenden decided as he headed back to engineering. He wouldn't apologize.

After all, he was right.

* * *

Lyssa Campbell was grateful she was alone in the turbolift as she headed back to the bridge. Her solitude gave her space to fume uninterrupted.

How dare that upstart puppy imply that those who served on *Voyager* were somehow "less Starfleet" than those who'd been in the Alpha Quadrant! This was his first time on a starship, for crying out loud. What did he know about it? What did he know about anything?

She thought back to the awful moment when she awoke in the transporter room alone, blood clotting in her hair, right after the Caretaker had abducted—there was no other word for it—*Voyager*. Learning that so many of her friends had been killed in an instant. Hearing the news that Janeway had deliberately destroyed the ship's one chance of getting home. The pain of that had been dreadful, but as time passed, Campbell found herself glad that Janeway had made that choice. She'd gotten to know Kes, the Ocampa, and the thought of that sweet girl being the last one of her species alive because of something *Voyager* had done . . . No. Such a thing was unthinkable. Janeway had made the right decision.

As the deck levels sped by, Lyssa thought of the friends she'd lost since then. Their faces crowded in her mind. There were so many—too many.

How dare David Chittenden say he'd suffered more.

She blew out a breath, stirring her blond hair, as the anger ebbed. Everyone had suffered, whether they were in the Alpha Quadrant or the Delta Quadrant. It was stupid to play this "we hurt worse than you did" game, but she knew that she and Chittenden were not the only ones playing it.

The war was over. *Voyager* had made it home. It was time to move on.

If only everyone agreed.

Campbell had to smile to herself as she realized that the only reason David Chittenden was getting to her so badly was because she liked him, and if she was any judge of men, he liked her too. Perhaps it was just as well they'd gotten off to so lousy a start. Shipboard romances were not usually a good thing.

Somewhat calmer, she returned to her station. No one had manned ops while she was on her lunch break; Harry was there and could have stepped in if anything had happened. No one knew ops better than Harry. Chakotay sat in his command chair, scrutinizing the computer. He glanced up as she entered.

"How was lunch?" he asked politely.

"Fine, sir, thank you."

"You're back early. You can take your full break if you'd like, Lieutenant." He indicated the image on the screen of stars streaking past. "It's not as if we're on red alert."

"Thank you, sir, I prefer to be at my station."

Chakotay smiled at her, but his eyes searched hers for a moment. She colored slightly under his scrutiny.

"As you wish, Lieutenant. Can't say I'm not happy

to have you here. Mr. Kim, you have the bridge, I'll be in my ready room," he said.

Kim moved down toward the captain's chair. Lyssa deftly touched a few buttons at ops and frowned slightly. She looked around; Kim was the highest ranking officer present, and they were old friends. She didn't like to reveal her ignorance, but she trusted him.

"Harry—excuse me, Lieutenant Kim?"

"Yes?" He looked over at her.

"Anything happen while I was gone?"

"Nope. All quiet. Why do you ask?"

"Nothing," she said quickly. "It's just . . . well, never mind."

Kim smiled. "Bet it's a ghost."

"A what?"

"A ghost. Something that's not really there. That happens a lot after a ship's undergone extensive work. You'll see something that looks out of the ordinary, and then when you try to check it, poof, it's gone."

"Yes, that's exactly what's happening," Campbell said, relieved.

Kim shook his head. "They really did a job on *Voyager*. They'd pretty well gutted her when we came aboard a few months ago."

"Plus they removed all your futuristic technology," said Tare, from the conn.

"Yeah, more's the pity," Kim said. The door to the bridge hissed and Ellis stepped out of the turbolift. Instantly, everyone tensed and returned their attention to their jobs. The lighthearted banter evaporated like water on a hot day. Kim quickly yielded his chair and returned to his station.

Lyssa stifled a sigh. She hoped Priggy would learn to loosen up. And, she thought, she hoped the rather priggy David Chittenden would too.

Chapter

8

CHAKOTAY NOW HAD a goal: to get the crew comfortable with him and with one another, at least somewhat, by the time they completed their mission. He'd take it section by section, dropping in, learning names and faces, and doing whatever he could to put his crew at ease. His first stop was engineering.

It was strange not to see—or hear—B'Elanna, he thought as he stepped off the turbolift. He missed his old friend, but knew that Vorik was a more than adequate successor. Vorik was finishing up a conversation with someone when Chakotay stepped behind his chief engineer and cleared his throat.

"Captain," said Vorik, turning smoothly, "what a surprise." He did not look surprised. Chakotay wondered if he ever did. "What can I do for you, sir?"

"I'd like to see your crew, see how you're doing. And I wanted to stretch my legs." From Vorik's expression, this was clearly not an adequate explanation, but then again, Chakotay was the captain. He didn't have to give adequate explanations.

"How is *Voyager* operating with its recent adjustments?" Chakotay asked.

Vorik's slanted eyebrows drew together in the closest approximation of resentment and disapproval Chakotay had ever seen him display.

"It was illogical to remove the technology," he said. B'Elanna had shared Vorik's sentiments, and Chakotay wished she could see the look on Vorik's face right now. The two chief engineers had more in common than he'd thought.

"For what it's worth, I agree with you," Chakotay said. "But neither of us is part of Starfleet Command."

When *Voyager* had returned home, the well-traveled ship had been the focus of intensive study. Sporting Borg modifications as well as technology from a future Starfleet, she had been gutted, stripped, and analyzed. All the "extraneous technology," as the stiff-faced admiral who authorized their removal referred to *Voyager*'s additions, had been confiscated. *Voyager* was now nothing more—and, Chakotay mentally amended, nothing less—than a standard *Intrepid*-class starship.

The reason given for this was twofold and contradictory: Starfleet needed to study the modifications, and Starfleet needed to remove the modifications so as not to pollute the timeline.

It was, as Vorik had said, illogical. But it was not unexpected.

"As painful as this may sound to a chief engineer," said Chakotay, "a ship is more than its technological components. *Voyager* was special because of her crew, and what we underwent together. Now that there's a different crew, she'll still be special and unique, but in a new way."

"It would have assisted this special and unique crew if the ship had been permitted to keep its special and unique technology," Vorik replied.

"Vorik," Chakotay said, grinning, "if you don't watch out, you'll develop a sense of humor one of these days."

Vorik looked slightly taken aback. "I sincerely hope not, sir."

Unable to help himself, Chakotay clapped him on the shoulder. He could have sworn Vorik winced.

"Come on. Introduce me to your staff."

Vorik obliged. Most of them were former *Voyagers*, so it was more a matter of getting reacquainted rather than introduced, but there was one newcomer.

"Ensign David Chittenden," the young man said, standing stiffly at attention.

"Oh, the whiz kid," said Chakotay. Chittenden

cringed, almost imperceptibly. "Vorik mentioned you. We're lucky to have you. Welcome aboard *Voyager*. This is your first assignment on a starship, isn't it?"

"Yes, sir," said Chittenden. He didn't meet Chakotay's eyes and looked a bit uncomfortable. Chakotay wondered why. He thought of himself as a pretty good judge of people, and Chittenden's demeanor struck him as more than rookie nerves. Chittenden's résumé was outstanding, and Chakotay knew all the engineering staff to be friendly and approachable people. Why, then, did they all seem to be standing somewhat apart from the newcomer? Bad blood already? He hoped not.

"You're in good hands," Chakotay said kindly. "I'm sure your fellow engineers are doing everything they can to make you feel welcome."

He eyed them meaningfully. Whatever had happened between Chittenden and the other engineers, he wanted them all to get over it.

"Of course, sir," said Chittenden. "It's a privilege to serve."

Chakotay wondered if he really meant it.

Voyager had one stop before it could head to its final destination, Deep Space 6. There was someone else who needed to be included in the mission. Janeway had described the person as a "spiritual adviser," someone who could work with Astall in helping the colonists adjust to resettling in a place they had left under such unhappy circumstances. Despite his own spiritual nature, Chakotay had questioned the need for this adviser.

"Surely whatever the colonists personally believe, there's someone in their group who would be better able to assist them than a stranger," he had said one evening over coffee at Janeway's apartment.

"The colonists with that kind of training chose to stay behind on Loran II," his friend and former captain had replied. "They asked for someone like this, someone who could empathize with them in a more spiritual capacity than a counselor might. This is an important mission, Chakotay. Starfleet wants to make sure the colonists feel that their every need has been met."

Chakotay had been unable to get a name from Janeway; she said that Starfleet hadn't decided yet. It would depend on who was available.

So it was with mild curiosity that Chakotay was in the transporter room when the so-called spiritual adviser beamed up. Ensign Thomas Stefaniak, who had taken over Lyssa Campbell's position as transporter operator, manipulated the controls and the adviser materialized on the platform.

Chakotay's jaw dropped.

"Surprise!" his baby sister said, her eyes bright and her grin threatening to split her face.

He caught her up in a big hug. "Sekky! That cunning Kathryn," he said when he released her. "You and she had this planned all along, didn't you?"

"Yep," Sekaya confessed smugly, looking completely unashamed. Grinning, Chakotay shook his head, taking it all in. He was aware of Stefaniak trying and failing to stifle his curiosity.

Chuckling, Chakotay said, "Ensign Stefaniak, this is my sister Sekaya. Apparently she's going to be a spiritual adviser to the colonists."

"Pleased to meet you, ma'am," Stefaniak replied, smiling. "Welcome aboard *Voyager*."

"Delighted to be here," Sekaya replied. "So, how's my big brother doing as captain? Has he gotten you all into any trouble yet?"

"You don't have to answer that, Stefaniak," Chakotay said quickly.

"Thank you, sir," Stefaniak replied, looking vastly relieved.

"Come on, Sekky. I'll show you to your quarters." They left the transporter room and headed for the turbolift. "Why didn't you tell me anything about this when I visited a few months ago?"

Sekaya was still chuckling at Chakotay's surprise as she replied, "My shamanic training wasn't finished, and I wasn't sure if it really was something I wanted to do. Besides, you had only just gotten home. We didn't want to drop everything on you at once. And then right after your visit, well, you suddenly got very busy saving the Federation. Again."

He grinned and ruffled her hair. "It's really good to see you," he said sincerely.

"You too, brother."

Sekaya was a gorgeous woman, tall, slim but curvaceous, with bright, intelligent eyes. The two were often mistaken for twins. They were only a year apart in age and resembled one another a great deal. There had been a deep and easy fondness between them while they were growing up, and Chakotay often wondered if his "contrary" nature, which had caused him to be the first person of Dorvan V to permanently leave the planet, had influenced Sekaya. While he was gone, after their father's death, she, too, had chosen to leave their home. That much he knew. What he hadn't known was why she had left.

"So tell me about this spiritual adviser position. Are you part of Starfleet?" he asked.

"No," she answered swiftly. "I've kind of created this position for myself. After you ran away and joined Starfleet," she said teasingly, "I started thinking about my own role on Dorvan V. I ended up assisting the shamans and getting my training from them, but I felt a strong need to take that knowledge elsewhere. Take it out to a wider circle."

"You contrary, you."

"Hey, that's your title," she joked back. Sobering a bit, she continued. "I felt that what I had learned needed to be shared, that there were others who were hungry for this. So, with the shamans' permission, I left and started training in other paths as well."

Chakotay was a bit startled at the revelation that his people's shamans were so forward-thinking.

"They approved of your sharing their secrets?"

"Not all of our secrets, no, of course not. But some things, yes. And many of them agreed with me that while it was important to keep our traditions alive and well within our tribes, it was time for someone to go out and share the richness of our path."

Chakotay looked at her with new respect. "Very good, Sekky. I'm proud of you."

She smiled, then said, "Not to be rude, but can you keep the nickname between us? I'm all grown up now, in case you hadn't noticed, and I prefer to be called Sekaya."

It was a mild rebuke, but a rebuke just the same, and Chakotay was surprised by how much it stung. For the first time, he was made sharply aware of the years that had passed between them, and just how far apart they had grown. The thought saddened him, but Chakotay supposed such things were inevitable.

"Of course, Sekaya."

Then she grinned, slipped an arm around his waist, and hugged him.

"But I hope I'll always be Sekky to you."

After they had gotten her settled in her quarters, Chakotay took Sekaya on a tour of the ship.

Her first visit was to Counselor Astall, with whom she

would be working closely on the mission. Upon being introduced, Astall made a happy sound and enveloped her "sister" in a bone-crushing hug. For the briefest instant Sekaya tensed, then she surrendered to the embrace, contentment stealing across her lovely features.

"I've always wanted to meet a Huanni," she said as they parted. "I have so much respect for the approach you bring to traditional therapy."

Astall ducked her head, pleased and slightly embarrassed by the words.

"We help heal by listening," she said. "It's surprisingly simple. While it comes naturally to our species, others seem to have a harder time of it. When we combine this deep listening with more traditional therapy, recovery time is greatly speeded up."

Chakotay frowned. He knew all this, of course, but for some reason the way Astall phrased it reminded him of something. He couldn't quite grasp it, and shrugged it off. It would come to him eventually.

Next, she met Kaz, who seemed utterly captivated by her, and then Fortier, who actually bent and kissed her hand. Colonist or no, his Gallic chivalry was intact. Chakotay thought wryly that the male colonists might spend more time in "counseling" with the beautiful Sekaya than with Astall.

When he took her up to the bridge, Sekaya greeted everyone with equal warmth, from the newcomer Tare to Kim to Ellis. Ellis shook her hand and glanced from her face to Chakotay's in mild surprise.

"You have the exact same features," he said, then added, "Although they look much better on you, ma'am."

Chakotay raised an eyebrow as Ellis met his eyes. It wasn't hard to read their expression. Ellis was doing his best to "loosen up," as Chakotay had suggested, and was clearly hoping he had not overstepped. Chakotay gave him an easy grin and a clap on the shoulder, and Ellis relaxed visibly. It was a good start.

In his quarters, Chakotay replicated some traditional foods grown on Dorvan V, and the two siblings had a feast. He deliberately kept the conversation light as he sensed Sekaya was holding something back.

Over coffee and dessert, a decadent chocolate cheesecake, Chakotay decided it was time to probe a bit further.

"Sekaya," he began, feeling his way, "I think there may be something we need to discuss."

He caught her in mid-bite. She'd just placed a forkful of cheesecake in her mouth and her eyes went wide as she chewed. Swallowing, she coughed, said, "Discuss what?" and reached for her coffee.

"Earlier today," Chakotay continued, "you said, 'We didn't want to drop everything on you at once.' "

He was right. Sekaya had been holding something back. She quickly looked down at her plate of half-eaten cheesecake. Then she flashed a smile at him.

"I should have known that you'd pick up on that. Just because you're a contrary doesn't mean you're slow on the uptake."

"Tell me."

She sighed and pushed her plate away. For a long moment, she stared at her hands, then she began.

"First, tell *me* your impression of how things were back home when you came to visit," she said.

Uneasily, Chakotay said, "Everything seemed fine. I asked around a bit, about how you fared under the Cardassians, and everyone reassured me that the occupation had gone quite uneventfully. That the Cardassians hadn't bothered you, as we had all hoped. I remember thinking that Father had died for nothing after all, that he must have gone out looking for a fight just on principle."

She eyed him. "Our father. A staunch proponent of peace and cooperation. You really believed he went looking for a fight?"

"It was the only theory I could come up with that fit the facts," Chakotay said. "If Dorvan V was never bothered by the Cardassians, and Father still joined the Maquis, what else was I to think?"

"When he died, you left Starfleet. You became a Maquis, just like him. You went looking for a fight just on principle too."

He looked down at his cup of cooling coffee. "Of course, the reason he and I hadn't spoken in so long was because I wanted to leave our world and join Starfleet. Father felt that Starfleet—that the Federation—had let our people down. When I got the news . . . it was almost as if Starfleet had killed him, as if *I* had killed him. So I picked up the torch he'd dropped. I picked up his cause. And I wear this in honor of him," he said, touching the tattoo on his forehead with a finger. "As do you."

She smiled, then the smile faded as she continued. "But . . . you didn't fight near our world," she said.

"No," he said. "The Cardassians were the enemy everywhere. I fought where I could—where I was sent."

"It must have been a relief to hear that the war was over, that the Maquis were all pardoned."

"It was, as I told you when I visited," he said, growing slightly annoyed. "Sekaya, you're dancing around the issue. What's all this about?"

Sekaya sighed. "Chakotay, we lied to you. Well, no," she amended immediately, "that's not true. We just . . . we just didn't tell you certain things."

"Things like what?"

"We haven't told anyone yet. The Federation abandoned us. We had no wish to tell them what we endured."

Concerned, he said, "What happened?"

She lifted her dark eyes to his. He saw her swallow. "Father didn't die for nothing. He didn't go looking for a fight. The fight came to us. You see . . . the Cardassians didn't leave us alone after all."

He reached across the table to clasp her hand. "Tell me."

"I will. It was one of the things I wanted to do, why I agreed to this mission when Admiral Janeway suggested it. But I didn't think— I just got here today, Chakotay. I want to tell you, but . . . I'm sorry. I'm just not ready to talk about it." She smiled without humor. "Maybe I should go see Astall along with the colonists."

"Maybe you should," he said, completely seriously.

Sekaya rose and tossed the napkin on the table. "It's late, and it's been a long day. I ought to get back to my quarters," she said.

"You can't just drop that on the table and walk away," Chakotay replied.

"I need more time to prepare. To figure out how to word things properly." She stood, twisting her fingers, staring at the carpeting. "I didn't expect to have to talk about it the first night. I thought we'd spend some time together, and it would just naturally come up."

"It just did."

She threw him a look of exasperation and fear commingled. "I know, but I just don't want to talk about it right now, all right?"

"Sekaya, you may not be part of Starfleet, but you're on a Starfleet vessel and I'm its captain. You've just told me that the Federation failed to protect our people. I'd be within my rights to order you to tell me."

Her dark eyes flashed. "You wouldn't," she said in a low voice.

He softened. "No, I wouldn't. But this . . . this isn't kind of you, Sekaya."

She went to him then and, bending, kissed his temple right on the tattoo.

"It's not about being cruel or kind, Chakotay. It's

about being ready to talk about something that's very important—to bare my soul. To reveal a secret. You know what a big thing that is to our people. And besides, I really did want to come on this mission to help the Loran II colonists. I don't want what happened to our colony to distract me from my duties to this one. Do you understand?"

He pressed her hand to his cheek. "Not really," he admitted. "But I respect you. Tell me when you feel the time is right, but I warn you, I'm not dropping you back off at Deep Space 6 without learning this secret."

She smiled then, and he felt relief wash over him as he saw the familiar dimple appear in her smooth brown cheek. Whatever it was, and it was clearly bad, it hadn't robbed his beautiful, ebullient sister of her ability to laugh. And for that, he was grateful.

"Thanks, big brother. The dinner was great. Good night." She paused at the door. "Chakotay . . . it really is good to see you again."

The door hissed closed behind her. He tossed his own napkin on the table and stared at it unseeingly, his hands on his hips.

"Everything seemed fine," he said to himself.

Chapter
9

Kaz whistled as he updated some files, pausing now and then to glance around appreciatively at his new surroundings. It had been a while since he'd been on a ship, and he liked what he saw of *Voyager*'s sickbay. Like nearly everyone in the medical profession, he'd read about the Doctor's "adventures" with interest and, truth be told, quite a bit of envy. To be a doctor in the Delta Quadrant, facing new challenges nearly every day—how stimulating such a thing must have been.

He chuckled to himself, wondering if that was really Jarem's thinking or Gradak's, or maybe even the poet Radara's. He was all of these, and yet he was his own man. Jarem very much enjoyed being a joined Trill, and not for the first time thought how fortunate he had been.

The whistling died in his throat as he recalled the circumstances under which that joining had come about. Most joined Trill who were about to receive a symbiont transplant lay beside the dying former host, so he knew his experience was not unique. But this had been no peaceful passing. Gradak hadn't wanted to die, hadn't needed to die.

Shouldn't have died. . . .

"Medical emergency," came the voice of Captain Lanham. *The ship was already on red alert.* *"Sickbay, prepare to receive injured."*

"Understood," snapped Jarem, running his hands under the sanitizing light. *"How many?"* His team began preparing even as he spoke, readying tricorders, assembling medications, prepping the biobeds, opening overflow cots.

"Sixteen," came the reply.

Kaz didn't ask who the injured were, where they had come from, how they came to be wounded. He didn't care. There would be time for that later. Right now, he was a doctor, and all that mattered was healing them if he could.

He heard the hum of the transporter. The wounded filled all the beds and some materialized on the floor. Quickly he and the nurses helped these to the cots. Some of the injured were conscious, with only minor injuries that Jarem's experienced eye recognized as being caused by phaser fire. Others were in much worse shape.

The transporter hummed again and more patients materialized. Jarem went cold inside as they shimmered into existence.

"Oh no," he breathed, sickened by the sight. Lying on the floor, burned and bloody, were several children. What had happened to them? What kind of depraved being would direct phaser fire on children?

He barked orders for a triage setup. His team assessed the injuries and immediately got to work on the worst of the injured. Even as he concentrated on setting up a blood infusion for a Bolian, he took a quick mental inventory of the races: mostly human, a few Bolians, and some Bajorans.

And then he understood. These were Maquis. But Maquis who had their families with them. . . .

"Doctor, you'd better see this," came a strained voice from one of his nurses.

"What?" he snapped as he monitored the Bolian. Good, he was stabilizing now that Jarem had hooked him up to the plasma infusion unit and closed his wounds with an autosuture. When the nurse didn't reply, Jarem turned around irritably—and went pale.

Clad in the odd, mismatched clothing typical of the Maquis and lying unconscious on one of the cots was a Trill.

Jarem's mouth went dry. He motioned to one of the nurses to finish up with the Bolian. Quickly, Jarem scanned the Trill. His injuries were extensive; he would not survive. Worse, he was joined. Both the host and the symbiont were in danger of death now.

Kaz licked his lips. "Computer, activate the Emergency Medical Hologram."

The balding, slightly annoyed-looking hologram appeared. "Please state the nature of the medical emergency."

"We have a joined Trill who's not going to make it," Kaz said. *"You have to remove the symbiont and prepare it for transport to Trill." Briefly, Jarem pressed the dying Trill's hand, then turned his attention back to the other patients.*

Sighing as if he were being dreadfully put upon, the EMH scanned the Trill.

"The symbiont has been traumatized," he said in a crisp, impersonal voice. "It will not survive the trip. You are correct in your assessment that the host also will not survive." Perfunctorily, he pulled a sheet over the still-breathing Trill and eyed the room full of injured. "Perhaps I can assist elsewhere."

"No!" cried Jarem, horrified at the Doctor's lack of compassion and startling himself and his team with his outburst. He ripped off the sheet from the injured man and stared again at the dying Trill's face. In a very real sense, this was his brother. Instilled in his people was an intense desire to protect the symbionts who were the keepers of what it truly meant to be Trill.

He couldn't stand here and watch both host and

symbiont die needlessly. Not when there was something he could do.

He made his decision. He wouldn't inform his captain, because regardless of what Captain Lanham said, Jarem knew he'd go through with his plan. Sometimes it was better to ask forgiveness than permission. He began to remove his uniform.

The hologram stared disapprovingly. "What are you doing, Doctor?" it inquired acidly.

"I'm getting ready for surgery," he said. "And I order you to do the same. You're to transfer the symbiont into me. I'm going to be its new host."

The hologram arched an eyebrow. "You are far too old to complete the joining successfully," it said.

"Not too old to try," Jarem said. Forestalling the hologram's next comment, Jarem said quickly, "In your expert medical opinion, can this man survive?"

"No."

"Can the symbiont survive the trip back to Trill without a host?"

Uneasily, the EMH replied, "No."

"Are the odds of its survival increased if it is transferred to a living host?"

Something flickered in the dark eyes. "Yes, provided both it and the host survive the transfer."

Jarem glanced around sickbay. His staff had everything under control. Those who had been most grievously wounded had already received treatment. They would survive; Jarem's team did not need his assistance.

The dying Trill did.

He pushed one of the emergency cots closer to the Trill Maquis. The man was still breathing, although barely.

Jarem looked up at the hologram. "May I remind you," the hologram said, "that you have not been properly prepared to accept the symbiont? That, in fact, you may prove to be a poor match?"

"Even a poor match increases the likelihood that the symbiont will survive, at least long enough to get it back to its homeworld," Jarem said. "Doctor, you're under orders from the chief medical officer to perform this surgery, so let's get going."

Suddenly he grinned. "I'll probably be court-martialed for this. That should make you happy."

"I am an Emergency Medical Hologram," it replied somewhat testily. It pressed a hypospray to Jarem's throat. The last thing Jarem heard as an unjoined Trill was the hologram saying irritably, "Happiness is irrelevant to the performance of my duty. Let us hope you survive long enough to warrant a court-martial."

Kaz smiled in remembrance. Captain Lanham had not pressed charges; after all, Jarem Kaz had not directly disobeyed an order. Plus, Kaz had argued very persuasively that his action had saved a life.

The first few weeks with the symbiont were difficult, more difficult than he had anticipated. The joining demanded a great deal of energy, and Jarem had to admit that he was indeed not as young as he once was. Lanham had wanted to cancel the ship's current mission and get Kaz to Trill, but Jarem had insisted he could manage.

And indeed, once that initial period had passed, he had proved to be a more than adequate host for the Kaz symbiont. He had learned so much from it about Gradak, the previous host, and all the others the symbiont had joined with. All of them were living within him now, after a fashion.

And Gradak's memories were swimming to the forefront now that they were on a mission heading back into what was once Cardassian space.

The door hissed, and Kaz returned to the present. He was surprised and pleased to see the ship's pilot standing awkwardly in his sickbay.

"Hello, Lieutenant Tare," he said. "What can I do for you?"

She glanced around, her dark eyes flickering.

"I have been told that I should report to you for a physical. I thought it best to get it over with."

Her body language, words, and tone of voice all screamed to him that she had no desire to be here. He couldn't blame her and was in fact surprised that she had taken the initiative. There were a few crew members he had suspected he'd have to chase down in order to get them to come in for their SOP physicals, and she topped the list.

"Please, get on the biobed. This won't take long." He gestured, and she hopped obligingly onto the bed.

The biobed ran through its analysis, then Kaz asked her to sit up while he examined her himself. He attempted to make small talk.

"How do you like *Voyager* so far?"

"So far, so good," she replied.

"Good people," Kaz ventured.

"Yes, it seems so."

"How have you been feeling overall?"

"Fine."

Not exactly forthcoming. She seemed to sense that he was probing, and she didn't appear to like it.

Akolo Tare was a special case. In keeping with Starfleet confidentiality, few of her current crewmates knew about her ordeal at the hands of Oliver Baines's holograms. Only Kaz, Astall, and Chakotay had been officially briefed about the incident. After she had been returned, Tare had undergone a thorough physical and psychological exam and been deemed fit to return to duty.

That was all Chakotay needed to know, but Kaz had a concern that the captain of *Voyager* didn't. Words and phrases from Tare's medical report floated back to him: *Subcutaneous hematomas present on both forearms and shoulders . . . some apparent erythema . . . indication of disruption at the cellular ATP or possibly mitochondrial level . . . moderate soft tissue abrasions . . . superficial lacerations . . . small areas of contusions and ecchymosis over labia . . . Etiology of trauma indeterminate, possibly secondary to sexual assault or other causes.*

In other words, Kaz thought bitterly, the doctor could neither confirm nor deny if Akolo Tare, in addition to being abducted, humiliated, and beaten, had also been sexually assaulted. Tare herself had volunteered no information either way.

If she had indeed been raped, it was a bad business, for more than the first and most pressing reason. Obviously, the most important thing was that Tare needed to come to terms with it sooner rather than later. She needed to heal emotionally as well as physically.

Also, Kaz knew it would shake the holographic rights issue to the core. Questions would arise that would need to be addressed: Did a hologram qualify as a person under these circumstances? Could it properly be called "rape" if the perpetrator wasn't a living being, but a collection of protons?

He was worried about her, but was unsure as to how to get her talking. After finishing his analysis, Kaz had an idea.

He looked at the tricorder and frowned. "There's nothing like good old-fashioned tactile input to help along technology," he said, extending his hands. "May I?" He wanted to see how she would react to a male touch.

Tare tensed. "Is that really necessary?"

"Strictly speaking, no," said Kaz. He kept his face bland, but watched her like a hawk. He didn't lie to his patients. "But," he continued, again telling the truth, "it would help me in my analysis."

"Do you suspect there might be something wrong?" she challenged.

He hesitated before replying, then decided that full disclosure was the best option. Akolo Tare didn't look like someone who appreciated the roundabout method of approaching things.

"Yes," he said finally, looking her right in the eye. "I suspect you might have been raped, Lieutenant."

Lieutenant Tare went very still. Her dark brown eyes never left his, but her nostrils widened as her breathing quickened. When she spoke, her voice was icy and calm.

"Have you completed the physical, Doctor Kaz?"

"Yes."

"Then I'm out of here."

She slipped off the biobed and strode purposefully toward the door.

"Lieutenant Tare," he called after her, "you didn't want me to touch you even in a professional manner during the course of a routine medical exam, and I'm a doctor and a flesh-and-blood being."

"What's your point?" she snapped, not breaking stride.

"What would you do if something happened to me? If you had to be treated by the Emergency Medical Hologram?"

She had reached the door. "I'd do whatever it took."

"Lieutenant!" Kaz heard a note of pleading in his own voice. She stopped at the door, but didn't turn around. Her body language screamed her conflict.

"Listen," Kaz continued, more softly. "The captain, Astall, and I are the only ones who know about your abduction. And only Astall and I were alerted to a possible sexual assault."

She turned her head and looked over her shoulder at him, carefully controlled anger on her beautiful face.

"Let's keep it that way," she said, and left.

It had been a lousy shift in engineering. Chittenden had encountered cold stares and icy voices the entire time. One expected that from Vorik, but not from fellow humans. He wondered if his argument with Campbell was now public knowledge. He hadn't meant to sound off like that—certainly not to a higher-ranking officer like Campbell—but it had hurt to be reminded of his friends who'd died defending the quadrant.

So when his shift ended, he hurried out of engineering and headed for the turbolift with more haste than was perhaps advisable. He could almost feel Vorik's eyes boring into him as he strode briskly for the door. *Let him stare,* David thought. He couldn't wait to get to his quarters and kick back with a good book, his favorite pastime.

The turbolift doors hissed open and he found himself staring into a pair of gorgeous blue eyes.

He couldn't speak.

"Are you getting on or not?" said Lyssa Campbell.

He wasn't sure. Which would be worse, riding with her or pretending he hadn't meant to get on the turbolift?

The former would be uncomfortable, but the latter would be just stupid. Looking down at the floor, Chittenden shuffled into the turbolift and gave it the floor he wanted.

The silence was agony. David racked his brain for something to say. He came up with exactly nothing. Out of the corner of his eye he saw Campbell looking at him from time to time. She looked as though, she, too, wanted to say something.

Finally, David took a deep breath. "Lieutenant Campbell, I wanted——"

"Ensign Chittenden, the other day——"

They looked at one another and laughed a little.

"You first," Chittenden said.

"No, you."

"You outrank me," he pointed out pleasantly.

She grinned. She was absolutely stunning when she grinned; David had thought the phrase about someone's face "lighting up" was a cliché, but in Campbell's case it was true.

"You got me there. Ensign, I wanted——"

The turbolift came to a halt and the doors opened. The cute red-haired woman and the rangy fellow David remembered seeing in the mess hall during his moment of shame entered. Campbell eyed them and fell silent. They stepped between Chittenden and Campbell, and in a moment, the turbolift reached Campbell's floor. She left without a word. David watched her go. He thought about following her, but both the doors and the window of opportunity had closed.

"A lot of us liked what you said in the mess hall the other day," the fellow said. He stuck out his hand and Chittenden shook it. "Name's Rafe Sanderson."

"I'm Janine McKay," the girl said, also extending her hand. She held David's a bit longer than was necessary. "Some of us are tired of the way the former crew of this ship seem to think they're better than us."

"I don't think they think that," David said. "They just . . . have a different perspective. Besides, they're our crewmates now."

"Yes," Rafe said, "and I'm happy to obey their orders and work with them. But that doesn't mean I have to like them."

"Our shifts are over. We're heading to the holodeck and then the mess hall for dinner," Janine said. "Would you like to join us?"

David thought about Lyssa Campbell, about the book that was waiting for him in his quarters, and decided to hell with both of them. This was a new phase of his life. He was going to do some new things.

"Sure," he said. "I heard there was a program that was really popular on *Voyager*. We should check it out."

They arrived at the holodeck. David figured out which program he wanted, and the doors slid open to reveal a darkened French bistro. A lovely young woman was performing songs in French to the accompaniment of a piano, and an older but still attractive blond woman drifted about, greeting familiar guests. A tall, gaunt man lined up a shot on a pool table.

Just as David was starting to smile at the scene, Janine snorted. "They considered this fun? No wonder they're all walking around like they have something shoved—"

"How about the one I showed you last time?" Rafe suggested.

Janine brightened. "Yeah, that was great. Let's do that one."

"Computer," called Rafe, "End current program and run Sanderson 4 instead."

The scene shifted. Instead of a bistro, they now stood in an alien bar. The music was loud and abrasive, and the air thick with smoke. If this were a real place, Chittenden realized he'd have his lungs full of illegal substances, but this was only a re-creation. The room was dark, and it took his eyes some time to adjust.

He could make out some gaming tables. Dabo? He couldn't tell. Over in another corner of the room, someone uttered a string of angry words in a language David didn't understand. The person threw something down on the table and stood up. Across the table, someone else stood up too. Their chairs fell back. Someone stepped between the two and said something that apparently calmed them down, but David averted his eyes regardless. It wouldn't take much for a fight to break out here.

"Thirsty, angel face?"

David glanced down to see a woman that he knew to be an Orion slave girl. Her thick, wild hair was black and her perfect body a gorgeous shade of green. The words were coquettish, but even in the dim, smoky light David could see that her eyes were dangerous. Rafe had his arm around the tiny waist of a woman from a species David didn't recognize, but in her skimpy outfit, it wasn't hard to see that she had three breasts.

Janine, too, had a companion, a human male, tall, fair-haired, and powerfully built. He was bare to the waist, and sweat gleamed on his oiled skin. He handed her a drink and kissed her throat in one smooth motion.

Janine caught David staring. She laughed as the man progressed from throat to earlobe. "Isn't he great? I've named him Herbert."

"Herbert?" Chittenden said, choking slightly.

"He's so *not* a Herbert I thought it was funny," Janine said. "Try the Romulan ale, it's fantastic." She eyed him, grinning a little at his discomfort.

"Thirsty?" repeated the slave girl. The word was a demand rather than a question. The green Orion woman eyed him and curled her lips in a snarl that managed to be both frightening and erotic at the same time.

"Um, yeah, I'll have a beer," Chittenden managed. He felt a little ill. This was not the sort of "entertainment" he enjoyed. Because holograms weren't really people, there were few restrictions on what one could do with them. You weren't supposed to create holograms that looked like people you knew, but beyond that, they were just a collection of photons. But the thought that Rafe enjoyed creating a slave woman and a gigolo who looked prepared to do more than just flirt nauseated him.

This smoky, seedy, rather scary place was not his cup of tea. He'd liked Sandrine's. He'd wanted to talk with the pretty Janine in a private, dark place, while they engaged in a harmless pastime like pool and sipped fine wine or drinks with exotic names. But she seemed to be enjoying the holographic male's attention a bit more than she ought, and suddenly she didn't seem quite so cute.

David wished he'd followed Lyssa out and given her that apology.

A yell went up from the game table in the corner of the room. That fight had broken out after all. It was going to be a long evening.

Chapter

10

"KLINGON BUREAUCRACY IS worse than Starfleet's, and I thought that was pretty bad," Torres whispered to her husband as they followed Commander Logt up a seemingly interminable flight of twisting stone steps.

They had spoken with Logt several days before about obtaining permission to consult the ancient records. At first, their request had been summarily denied. To Tom's surprise it was B'Elanna who had challenged Logt and pushed back, insisting that they had a right to peruse any records that might pertain to their offspring. Logt had contacted them only that morning with the good news that the just-rebuilt library would indeed be open to them. With restrictions, of course.

"Well, at least we'll stay in shape," Paris whispered back to her, his legs burning from climbing the steps.

Logt paused, then turned menacingly. "Do you have a comment, Paris?"

Tom tried not to gulp and failed. "Not at all. Ma'am," he added.

Logt glowered, then turned and continued. B'Elanna glanced back at her husband, her eyes bright with suppressed mirth, and they both fought down illogical giggles.

Warmth flooded Tom. He loved this woman so much. He was more than willing to stick it out here on Boreth as long as she continued to blossom. And anything that was good for B'Elanna was good for their daughter, that excruciatingly precious little bundle of delight who was currently in Kularg's good Klingon hands.

He was, however, relieved when they reached the top of the stairs. Logt produced an ancient skeleton key from somewhere in the folds of her uniform, inserted it into a lock that was bigger than Tom's hand, and turned it.

Tom winced at the groaning sound the lock made, but the huge wooden door swung open. Logt stepped inside. Torres and Paris followed.

"Wow," said Tom, looking at row after row of ancient tomes. The huge bookcases extended from the floor to the extremely high ceiling and stretched so deeply into the room that Tom couldn't see how far they went. A rich smell teased his nostrils.

Books, he thought with a tinge of wonder. *That's the smell of books.*

He'd seen books before, of course, and appreciated them for the antiques they were. But most of the reading he'd done, and admittedly it hadn't been a lot, had been off padds. Paris wasn't much of a scholar, though he'd managed to get decent enough grades at the Academy. He preferred interactive novels on the holodeck to those one curled up with in one's quarters.

But even he could appreciate the years—make that centuries—of knowledge that were represented here. The sun came in through small apertures in the stone high above his head, casting pools of light upon the stone floor. Dust motes swirled languidly in the thick beams of light. There were huge, heavy tables and chairs, and wooden cabinets that competed with the bookcases.

"This is amazing," said B'Elanna. Both she and Tom had spoken in hushed whispers.

"I am pleased you appreciate the work of the ancient scholars," said Logt approvingly. "We were fortunate indeed that the books were spared during the attack. They have only recently all been placed here, in their new home. You will value them even more once you have read the words of the scholars, calling out to us across the centuries."

Tom usually didn't get into this sort of stuff, but his skin prickled at her words. As he continued to look around, two priests appeared, seemingly from nowhere. Despite their less martial attire, they looked—and Paris knew they were—every bit as formidable as Logt.

"Gura and Lakuur will assist you in acquiring the books and scrolls you need," Logt said. "I will return to my duties. You may visit here every day for an hour at this time. Do not attempt to gain access at any other time."

Without another word Logt departed, her bootheels ringing in the huge chamber. Paris heard the door close behind her with a resounding boom.

The priests stared at them with barely concealed dislike. Tom was really starting to get tired of the condescension with which the priests viewed him and, to only a slightly lesser extent, B'Elanna.

"You are the parents of the so-called *Kuvah'Magh*?" one of them—Tom wasn't sure if it was Gura or Lakuur—demanded, scowling.

"We are the parents of Miral Paris, whom a group of Klingons we encountered in the Delta Quadrant believed was their savior, yes," said B'Elanna.

One of the priests snarled. "Hmph. I wonder if, half human as you are, you understand the arrogance of your claim?"

"I claim nothing," B'Elanna said, jutting her chin out a bit. "I know that Kohlar and his people believed this to be true. I wished to see the documentation upon which they based their belief and any other scrolls or books that might be pertinent."

"A mongrel and a human in this sacred room," the other cleric muttered. "It is a sad state of affairs."

Tom choked back a retort and let B'Elanna handle it. At least she carried the same blood as they. She did not rise to the bait, merely stood her ground and gave them stare for stare. After a moment the priests shook their heads and led "the mongrel and the human" to a table.

"Logt notified us of the nature of your request. We have pulled the pertinent tomes and scrolls," one of them said. "Lakuur will show you how to touch them."

Well, at least we now know which one's which, Tom thought. Lakuur handed them each a pair of gloves. It was at that point that Tom realized something he ought to have figured out earlier. They were not going to be able to look at translations of these texts; they were going to have to handle the actual books themselves. His stomach flip-flopped.

"Put these on," Lakuur ordered. "You will be permitted to peruse one item at a time." He shook his index finger at them, emphasizing the number. "When you are done, ring the chime and I will return the tome to its proper place. If you wish to take notes, you may, but you must be careful. If the ink spills and damages one of the precious books, you will be ordered to leave Boreth and never return."

Tom now noticed the small, pointed piece of bone

on the table sitting next to an old-fashioned inkwell. Oh, great. This was just getting better and better.

Gingerly, he and B'Elanna put on their gloves and sat down with the first of the scrolls. Tom held his breath as B'Elanna slowly, carefully unrolled it. Fortunately, although it looked as though it might, it did not crumble to pieces. Tom took the sharpened piece of bone that was to serve as a pen and the ink and sat down beside her. A second later, he stood and moved several seats away from B'Elanna and the scroll. The more distance between the ink and the ancient, irreplaceable scroll, the better. Lakuur watched them for a moment, then grunted and left.

The minute he was gone, B'Elanna looked at Tom.

" 'Oh, honey, let's see what else is out there about the *Kuvah'Magh*.' Great idea," she said sarcastically.

"Well, I didn't know," he protested. "I thought we'd be looking at translated padds, for heaven's sake. I had no idea we'd have to wade through this." He gestured at the pile of books and scrolls.

"You get to take the notes," she said, "since you can't read Klingon." She perused the first scroll and her face fell. "Tom . . . I'm not sure even I can read this. It's Klingon, but it's a very archaic version."

"It would probably be like my trying to read Middle English," said Tom, his mind going back to when he was a teenager having to recite Chaucer's *Canterbury Tales. Whan that Aprill, with his shoures soote. . . .*

He marveled at the scrap of knowledge that floated up. Memory was a funny thing.

"Harder than that," mused Torres. She continued looking at the scroll. Then, softly, she smiled.

"This is it, Tom."

"This is what?"

She gestured at the parchment. "This is the scroll that Kohlar and the others made copies of. It was written shortly after Kahless made the Promise. The monk who experienced the vision and who wrote the prophecy was supposed to be one of the first sent to Boreth, but he apparently angered some of the wrong people. The scroll of the *Kuvah'Magh* was written while he was in exile. I'm surprised it even survived."

Tom picked up the bone writing implement, trying not to mentally identify its original owner. He dipped the sharp tip in the bowl of thick black ink and tried to write on the parchment that had been provided. He succeeded in creating a very large blot.

"This may take a while," he said to his wife.

"It's beautiful," said Sekaya, and meant the words.

She, Astall, Fortier, and some of the other colonists stood on a gently swelling ridge, looking over the colonists' former home. It was twilight, and the glorious hues of purple and orange bathed the simple yet functional houses that formed a small "town square." Surrounding the square, crops stretched out as far as she could see. There was no lack of technology available, but it was harmoniously integrated into the land-scape and it seemed to present to Sekaya a union of the best of both worlds.

"It's no wonder you wanted to return," breathed Astall, her hands clasped to her heart and her large eyes alight with wonder.

Fortier turned to them, his eyes searching each of their faces.

"This is why I wanted you to come with us tonight," he said. "I wanted you to see our home, so that you would understand."

Already some of the other colonists were venturing down the grassy slopes to the buildings they had called home. Birds twittered in the skies, settling down on trees to sleep for the night, while a baying, yipping noise in the distance indicated that there were others for whom the night was familiar.

Fortier stood with the counselor and the spiritual ad-viser on the knoll, the fragrant, warm wind tousling his hair. Sekaya noticed that his eyes were moist.

"Thank you for inviting us," said Sekaya. "This re-sembles my home."

"Perhaps one day, after we are well resettled, we can visit your colony," said Fortier. "It seems we share a great deal."

Sekaya was pleased. The holodeck re-creation was apparently a good one, if it made Fortier and the colonists so happy. Astall had recommended program-ming it so the colonists would have a taste of home before they arrived. And, she had shared with Sekaya, so both women could study how the colonists reacted and be able to head off any potential trauma.

But there seemed to be little potential trauma here. Fortier was eager, yet slightly melancholy; such was to be expected. Astall's ears were up and alert, swiveling as she followed the sounds of conversation. Later, she and Sekaya would try to talk to the colonists one-on-one and get their reactions.

"When my people arrived on Dorvan V," said Sekaya, "we hosted an elaborate ritual to introduce ourselves to the land. To greet and honor our new home."

She sat down on the grass and folded her arms over her legs, enjoying the peaceful scene spread out in front of her. After a moment, Fortier joined her.

"We consider ourselves fairly spiritual people, but we do not have an extensive background in ritual," said Fortier. "It sounds nice."

She turned to look at him. "We could design one for your return. It might help to integrate those who left with those who remained."

She deliberately did not give voice to the fear that they all harbored: that the colonists who remained might well be dead. No one knew what these people would be returning to. They might behold the same tranquil, pastoral vista that spread before them now, complete with their loved ones waiting to greet them. They might see total devastation; Loran II might have been the site of a battle during the war. It was simply an unknown.

Privately, Sekaya had spent much time alone in her room with her personal medicine bundle, sinking deep into meditation and planning a ritual for the worst-case scenario. The dead would need to be mourned, if dead there were. She did not mention this alternative plan to Fortier. There would be time enough to present it, gently and with compassion, if the need arose. Much better to have Fortier thinking about a joyful reunion.

Fortier's gaze was soft, appreciating the re-creation of his home as the day darkened to night. His full lips curved.

"That would be a pleasant thing indeed." His eyes returned to her, slightly wary. "But we do not follow your path, Sekaya."

"And I would not design a ritual that did," Sekaya replied. "This is all about what is important to you and your people, Mr. Fortier."

"Call me Marius," he said.

She smiled. "Marius, then. You lived on Loran II for many years. There was plenty of time for you to develop your own unique culture. Tell me what you enjoyed doing there."

Before Sekaya realized what was going on, Astall was on her feet, moving quickly down the hill. Looking down, Sekaya saw that one woman was wiping tears from her face while a friend tried to comfort her. They stood in front of a small house, which was probably the home of the weeping woman. Fortier tensed and made as if to rise, but Sekaya laid a gentle, restraining hand on his arm.

"Astall knows what she's doing," Sekaya reassured him. "Let her talk to Kara by herself. You can talk to her later if you like."

The muscles in Fortier's jaw worked, but he nodded. "We had no counselor available to us on Loran II," he said. "We're not used to it."

"She's a Huanni, and they're the best," said Sekaya. "We're all hoping that everything will be all right, Marius. But there's a chance that things might not be."

He looked at her then. "You were lucky," he said. "Your colony was ignored by the Cardassians. You escaped the war unharmed. I can only hope ours had the same fate."

Sekaya's chest contracted as if she had been physically struck.

"Yes," she said, her throat tight. "We were very lucky."

And her mind shouted, *Liar!*

Chapter

11

"HI," SAID KIM.

Libby's face broke into the dazzling smile that he so loved.

"Well, hi yourself," she replied. "How is everything, Chief of Security?"

"It's been pretty quiet around here," Kim admitted. "So far I haven't done a thing except stand at my station and look menacing."

She laughed at that; he had to smile along with her. He couldn't quite manage to be the impassive threat that Tuvok was, but he knew what he was doing.

"Maybe you'll acquire the menacing bit later," Libby said. "But seriously, Harry, fill me in. I miss you. What's going on?"

"Well," Kim said, "we're making our way to Loran II. The colonists seem like nice enough people, though everyone's a bit edgy."

Her face softened in sympathy. "If only you knew what happened," she said. "It must be awful for them, waiting and wondering."

"Yeah," said Harry, knowing that Libby knew exactly how hard waiting and wondering could be.

"How's Lyssa doing in your former position?"

"She's terrific, as you might expect." Lyssa and Libby had gotten to be good friends in the six months since *Voyager* had returned. "There's a fellow she's taken a shine to, but it sounds like he's being a bit of a jerk."

"Really? How so?"

"Well, when *Voyager* was lost in the Delta Quadrant, there was a bit of a clash between the former Maquis and those of us who were still with Starfleet," Harry said.

"I've met B'Elanna and Chakotay," Libby said, "and it sure looks as though whatever differences you had you've put behind you."

"Seven years in tight quarters will do that," Harry replied. "But now there seems to be some tension between those of us who were on *Voyager* and those who fought the Dominion War. It seems that some people who were here seem to think we were lucky for having missed it."

He tried to keep his voice conversational, but the bitterness crept in. And of course Libby, who knew him so well, didn't miss it.

"Oh, honey," she said, "someone said this to you?"

"To Lyssa," he said. "I told her she could write him up for it, but she doesn't want to. Says it would cause undue friction, and maybe she's right."

"I'm really sorry. This may work itself out over the course of this mission."

"Yeah, I hope so. It's not the best way to start out. How about you? What's on your plate?"

She rolled her eyes. "Oh, my gosh, *everything*. My agent has me playing in Australia next week, and then I'm doing something else on a starbase somewhere." She waved a hand absently.

Kim smothered a grin. Libby was intelligent and talented and drop-dead gorgeous, but she certainly wouldn't have cut it in Starfleet. "Starbase somewhere" indeed.

"I'm sure you'll do great," he said sincerely.

"Speaking of which . . . I'm sorry, but I really need to practice," she said.

"I've got a lot of stuff to do too," Kim said quickly. It wasn't exactly a lie, but he would much rather keep talking to her.

"I'm going to selfishly hope the rest of your mission is totally boring," she said, smiling.

"You do that." He paused. "I love you, honey."

"I love you too."

As her image disappeared, to be replaced by the familiar Starfleet insignia on the screen, Harry Kim thought, *Then why won't you marry me?*

Libby felt the smile fade from her face after she said good-bye to Harry. She wished with all her heart she could have said yes to his marriage proposal, but now was not the time. She had responsibilities that demanded her attention. The true irony of the situation was that the only thing keeping them apart was the fact that they were both devoted to serving the same organization heart and soul.

She took a break from work and let her mind wander as she got up and did some stretches. She thought back to the night when he had proposed.

Libby had convinced Harry to spend a few days with her in her beloved Maine, and they had had a wonderful time. On their last night, she took him to a small town called Castine that was rich in maritime history.

The weather had been beautiful. They had walked hand in hand past the eighty-five-foot elm trees that were among the oldest on the continent. A gentle breeze blew in from the harbor, bringing with it the smell of salt air and the cry of the gulls. They took the walking tour around the small town, and it seemed to Harry that every ten feet there was a monument or a house or a ruin or a plaque.

"Castine has been occupied for over seven hundred years," said Libby. "Explorers from Champlain to John

Smith have been here, and it figured in the American Revolution and the War of 1812."

On Battle Avenue, Libby paused at one house. "This is Abbot House, built in 1802," she said. "Abbot's bride didn't want to come here. When she did, she was greeted by a house with no front steps!"

Harry laughed. "That must have made it hard for Mr. Abbot to carry her over the threshold. These old houses and towns do have their stories, don't they?"

"Oh, that's just the start. At the Brown House on Perkins Street, the children in the 1800s reported seeing the face of a mad relative glowering at them from the ell window," Libby said. "And Fort George Park—right over there, near the Abbot House—was the site of the first public hanging in the county. They say," and her voice dropped to a whisper, "that on warm nights in August, if you listen very hard, you can hear the soft *rat-a-tat* made by the ghost of a drummer boy."

Libby had been trying to spook Harry a little, but it was she who squeaked a moment later when he unexpectedly went "Boo" right in her ear. Laughing, they continued on to Libby's favorite old house. "This is the Whitney House," she said. "It was occupied by the British for a while. An officer there scratched the American flag upside down and wrote 'Yankee Doodle Upset' on one of the windowpanes."

Harry laughed. "Where is it?"

"The windowpane? Broken, I'm afraid, in the late

1800s. Someone accidentally whacked it with the back of a shovel while clearing snowdrifts off the porch."

"Oh, that's too bad; I would have liked to have seen it. I guess nothing really lasts forever, not even in this town."

Libby was pleased with his delight. Castine, only a few square kilometers, took great pride in its history, and as Libby knew he would, Harry loved it. They ended at a church built in 1790 that featured a steeple designed by Charles Bulfinch and a genuine Paul Revere bell.

The Maine Maritime Academy had long since been closed, but remained open as a museum. Part of it consisted of a large holographic area.

"We have time to visit," Libby said. "You can participate in what's considered to be the worst naval defeat in United States history and find out what it's like to scuttle your ship."

Harry wrinkled his nose. "I don't think I'd want to know what it's like to have to scuttle my ship," he replied. "No, as much as I love holodeck simulations, I think I'll just enjoy the real thing here. It's harder to find."

As they walked the decks of the old *Pride of Maine*, Harry mused, "You know, Admiral Janeway told Captain Janeway that *Voyager* would become a museum one day."

Libby was confused. "I don't understand."

He laughed a little.

"Right before we came home. Remember I told you

about the time-traveling Admiral Janeway? She told her younger self that in her time, *Voyager* was a museum. Just like this ship has become."

"That's a sad thought. It's such a vibrant vessel, it's hard to think of it being decommissioned. But I guess it's inevitable. Better that than getting blown to bits in a battle, I suppose."

"It would all depend upon the reason for the battle," said Kim with just a touch of melodrama.

Libby went cold inside. Even the thought of losing him, now that she had gotten him back after thinking him dead for so long, was painful. She slipped her hand in his as they continued to walk the decks.

Changing the subject, she said, "Well, we certainly don't need a holoprogram to travel back in time here."

"No, we don't. This is an amazing place, Libby. Thank you for sharing it with me."

He bent and kissed her. She'd sensed something was up; she could tell by his kiss.

That night, they had dined at a place called the Castine Inn. Built in 1898, the building exuded quiet elegance. "The current owners are the descendents of the Mr. Vogel who built it," Libby had told Harry. They walked through the gardens, stepped up on the wraparound porch, and went inside. The dining room was a delight, with a mural of the town covering all four walls.

"Gorgeous!" exclaimed Harry. Having a captain who loved to paint had taught him an appreciation of art.

"It was painted way back in 1989," Libby said. "The really interesting thing is, this is the town exactly as you would have seen it at the time if there were no walls. It's a three-hundred-sixty-degree view. And all the people were real, too, known personally by the artist, Margaret Parker Hodesh."

Kim looked admiringly at her. "You really have done your research," he said.

"All a part of being a good guide," she replied.

The room was lovely, but it was the meal they had come for. Libby started with a butternut squash soup with saltwater cranberries for her appetizer, and Harry selected white truffle oil risotto with fresh herbs. They each had a salad of mixed greens and mushrooms with an olive oil and blueberry balsamic vinaigrette. For his entrée, Harry chose loin of lamb with pickled fiddle-head ferns—like nearly everything on the menu, a local delicacy—while Libby selected lobster. Looking rue-fully at the red crustacean on her plate, she explained to Harry, "This is the fellow who tempted me to add fish to my hitherto pure vegetarian diet. I couldn't live in Maine and not eat lobster."

For dessert, they decided to split a decadent-looking blueberry cobbler. When the server brought it out, Libby saw something shiny nestled in the whipped cream topping. She gasped, and both joy and regret flooded her.

Fishing out the diamond ring from the creamy whiteness and cleaning it with a napkin, Harry said,

"Well, maybe the whipped cream bit wasn't the best idea, but it sounded awfully romantic. Libby, will you marry me? I'd carry you over the threshold even if there weren't any stairs."

She had turned a stricken expression to him and had to endure the wrenching sight of disappointment flooding his sweet face. Libby was keenly aware that the waitstaff and even the inn's proprietors were lurking in the doorways, watching, ready no doubt to bring out a celebratory bottle of champagne. Why on Earth hadn't Harry done this in a more private fashion?

Because he had every reason to believe from your behavior that you would say yes.

She wanted to say yes.

"Harry, I—"

He swallowed hard. "It's okay. I'm sorry, I thought—"

She leaned forward and kissed him hard. Whispering in his ear, she said, "I love you so much, but I just want a little more time. This isn't a 'no,' it's a 'not yet.' "

He brightened a little at that, but nonetheless excused himself and went to talk to the waitstaff. They seemed disappointed. Libby felt her face turning bright red and stared at the napkin she was twisting into knots in her lap.

She was too miserable to do more than poke at the cobbler. They decided against coffee and returned to her cabin. He had made some excuse about needing to return to San Francisco, and she had pretended to believe the excuse. When he was gone, she threw herself on the bed in sheer misery. Her cats, Rowena and Indigo, cuddled up with her, offering what comfort they could.

If only she could tell him the real reason.

Libby shook herself out of her reverie and returned to her duty. Fletcher had tried to sweeten the blow with flattery, telling Libby that it was through her determined efforts that six months ago they had figured out what was going on in covert ops in time to stop it. The flattery hadn't worked; Libby still hated the grindingly boring tasks that made up so much of her work.

The one thing that did seem intriguing was the fact that while Mole—somehow she always thought of *The Wind in the Willows* when she used the term—had clearly accessed many different classified documents over the last few years, there didn't seem to be any corresponding leaks to the Cardassians, Vorta, or even the Syndicate. Mole was gathering information, that much was certain. He—or she—had even been able to access information that Aidan hadn't been privy to. And yet, there was no evidence that the information thus gleaned had been passed on to anyone.

She fell back on her tried and true method of puzzling something out. What were the facts?

One: Someone placed at least somewhat high in Starfleet was accessing documentation on an extremely classified level—including all of *Voyager*'s logs. That particular bit of information was one reason Libby suspected Fletcher wanted her in on this—he knew she had a personal investment in finding the mole.

Two: She or he had left a trail, but Libby couldn't assume it was a complete one.

Three: The information that Fletcher knew Mole had learned was not the usual sort of thing. In addition to documentation that pertained to the Dominion War, which was to be expected, Mole had been accessing medical data and research, little-known negotiations, and private personnel files. Vital information in the wrong hands, certainly, but hardly the sort of information that was usually sold on the black market. It seemed oddly intimate. Libby wondered if maybe Mole was trying to frame someone.

She shook her head. "Supposition, Agent Webber," she told herself firmly. She returned to her list of known facts.

Four: Mole was slippery. Every lead she'd followed had petered out. It almost seemed as though there were a lot of Moles with the same agenda, each one gathering just a little bit of information here and then absconding with it, never lingering too long lest he be caught. . . .

Now, there was a frightening thought, and the hairs on the back of her neck lifted as she pondered it.

What if there wasn't one mole? What if there was a whole group of them?

What if this was a real, honest-to-God conspiracy?

* * *

After his disappointing evening, the Doctor glumly returned to his apartment, which had been specially equipped with holographic emitters throughout. There was a message waiting for him. He scowled at the blinking light, as if it were the source of all his troubles, then he ignored it. He didn't care who it was. He didn't want to talk to anyone. Sighing heavily, he threw himself onto the couch, covered his face with his arms, and wallowed in his wretchedness.

"A dismal universal hiss, the sound of public scorn," he muttered, quoting Milton.

In all his years of activation, he had never been so spurned. Not even his time in prison compared to the anguish and humiliation he had endured over the last three hours. The worst thing about it was that he knew full well that none of it had been meant in malice. They weren't trying to make him feel dreadful—they just did.

His computer beeped again. He rolled over and covered his ears with the pillow.

"Go away and leave me to my misery," he muttered.

The beeping continued. There was only one person in the galaxy with that kind of stubborn patience, and even as he cringed from the thought of talking to her, he knew he wanted very much to see her face.

At last, steeling himself, he went to the computer.

"Doctor." It was, as he had known it would be, Seven of Nine.

"Seven," he said, imitating her stiff manner.

"It is my understanding that your speech was not well received."

He looked away. "I'd rather not talk about it, if you don't mind."

"I do mind. I am transporting over." And just that quickly the transmission ended and there was a hum in his living room.

The Doctor folded his arms and tried to look annoyed, but was too glad to see her for the pretense to be believable. He was always glad to see her, even though he saw her every day.

She was dressed in more casual clothes than she wore to their place of work, and she was wearing her hair loose. But her manner was as stiff as usual.

She got straight to the point.

"It has been my experience that for humans, a common way to acknowledge distressing passages in their lives is to participate in an activity called 'drowning their sorrows.' This usually consists of imbibing alcoholic beverages and interfacing with members of their collective who do not object to their somewhat maudlin behavior. Should you wish to acknowledge your disappointing reception among your peers this evening in such a ritual fashion, I will agree to accompany you."

"Somehow, I think that was intended to make me feel better," the Doctor said.

Seven arched a blond eyebrow.

"I don't drink, Seven," he said, both moved and exasperated by her. "I can't. Well, not the way you're referring to, anyway."

"Nonetheless, you have been known to exhibit maudlin behavior. I will tolerate it if it assists you in regaining your usual equilibrium. Our group needs you operating at full capacity if we are to continue to maintain our high standards of intellectual discernment and offer our full assistance to the Federation."

Four years since she was liberated from the Borg, and she still talks like a computer, the Doctor thought, somewhat fondly. Seven was Seven, and that was exactly why she was so dear to him.

"Very well," he said. "Let us go forth and drown our sorrows."

Chapter

12

THE DOOR CHIMED. "Come," called Astall.

Her easily readable face registered surprise as her door hissed open and Kaz stepped inside. She got to her feet immediately.

"Dr. Kaz!" she exclaimed. "How very nice to see you. What can I do for you?"

He didn't take the seat she indicated right away, but stood, fidgeting a little.

"I was wondering what your schedule looked like today," he said.

She narrowed her eyes and went to the replicator. "I'm just about to have a nice cup of *tranya*," she said. "Will you join me?"

"No thanks."

The cup of orange beverage materialized in the replicator and Astall took a sip. Her ears flapped gently as she closed her eyes in pleasure.

"I just *love* this," she said. She turned toward her guest. "My schedule is wide open," she said. "Are you inquiring for yourself or on behalf of a patient?"

Sighing, Kaz gave up the appearance of nonchalance and dropped into a chair. He rubbed his tired eyes.

"Myself," he admitted.

"Thought so," she said. "You look like you haven't been getting a lot of sleep."

"I've been having some very distressing dreams lately." He smiled without humor. "I'm such a hypocrite. There are a couple of people I've advised to come see you, and yet I keep putting it off myself."

Astall wrinkled her nose pertly. "You'd be surprised at how often that happens," she said. "Medical professionals, in both our fields, are often very good doctors, but very bad patients."

"When can I schedule an appointment?"

She shrugged. "I'm free now. Are you?"

His eyes widened slightly. He realized he had hoped he could just get away with the empty gesture of making the appointment and then "forgetting" to show up. Her eyes twinkled, and he realized that although she wasn't a telepath, she knew exactly what he was thinking.

He laughed self-deprecatingly. "Yes," he said. "I am."

"Computer," Astall said, "run privacy program Astall One."

"Request granted," came the pleasant voice of the computer. Now, Kaz knew, they would not be disturbed unless there was an emergency.

Astall rose and got a padd. She flicked a few buttons, then nodded. Gesturing with the padd, she said, "This is your record. Give me just a moment. . . ."

She settled into her chair, her large eyes flickering rapidly as she read. Kaz knew that she'd only have to read the information once. All Huanni were blessed with eidetic memories.

"Now," said Astall, setting the padd down. "Tell me about these dreams."

He clasped and unclasped his hands, not sure where to start. Finally, he just decided to plunge right in.

"They're about the life of one of Kaz's previous hosts. Gradak. He was a Maquis. He was one of those killed during the attack on Tevlik's moon."

"Oh, Jarem." Her voice was full of sympathy. "That was an awful incident. We on Huan mourned so deeply for the fallen." He heard the sincerity in her voice and felt warm inside.

"Well," Kaz amended, "Gradak wasn't killed then, exactly. But it was there that he received the wounds that he'd die from later, on my ship."

"Your ship? You weren't able to save him?"

Kaz shook his head. "That's not the point. We were able to safely transfer the symbiont to me. That's how I became joined. But he—I—we keep having these memories of the night when he was attacked."

She held up a pale purple hand.

"May I interrupt for a moment?"

"Certainly."

"I make it a point to learn as much as I can about the various species who serve with me," Astall said. "So I've done a lot of reading about your people, but of course I'm sure I haven't grasped everything. Now . . . correct me if I'm wrong, but don't Trill hosts undergo a great deal of training before they're joined with a symbiont?"

"Oh, yes. It's quite rigorous, being an initiate."

"And yet you just told me that you received your symbiont a few short years ago. As an older man, without any psychological preparation for the joining, and under extremely trying circumstances."

"That's right." Kaz nodded, wondering where this was leading.

"And right now, you're on a mission that is going to take you into what was formerly Cardassian territory."

"I thought that might have something to do with it," Kaz said, "and at first I just dismissed it. But then I . . . well, I started to get concerned when the dreams kept recurring. They were so vivid."

She smiled and shook her head.

"No need for concern, Jarem. But you're wise to address the problem before it grows worse. I have a feeling that these factors I just cited are combining to create an environment of stress for you at this point in time. I would imagine that it's hard enough to integrate the emotions of a symbiont under ideal circumstances. With no preparation whatsoever, you were forced to absorb the memories of someone who'd been killed in one of the worst, most despicable slaughters in Federation history. And your record says nothing about you taking any leave to return to Trill for any further counseling."

She looked at him a little sternly. Kaz was reminded of a teacher he'd had when he was a boy and smiled a bit sheepishly.

"No," he said. "I would have if there had been a problem, but after a few weeks everything seemed just fine. Neither my captain, who's the one who okays any leave, nor I felt there was a need. And it's not as if I haven't been under stress since I received the symbiont," he added.

"Of course not. But I'm willing to bet that subsequent stressors had nothing to do with being a Maquis, or being in Cardassian space. Or even being around a cluster of people who have chosen to strike out in a different direction."

That insight surprised Kaz. "You think the colonists are part of what's triggering these memories?"

"They're families of independent thinkers who live together in an isolated place far from normal Federation activity," she said. "Ring a bell?"

He nodded slowly. He should have seen that for himself. "Yes," he said. "Sounds an awful lot like the Maquis and their families hiding out on Tevlik's moon."

She smiled, her eyes soft with sympathy.

"No wonder Gradak is crying out to be heard," Astall said. "You've never performed the *zhian'tara*, have you?"

He shook his head.

"Why not?"

"I just . . . never got around to it."

He didn't look at her as he answered. The real truth was that the ritual, which temporarily transferred the personalities of the Kaz symbiont into the bodies of the current host's various friends, was a deeply personal one. The host had to completely trust the people he was permitting to bear the personalities. The Kaz symbiont had had twelve hosts, including Jarem; it had been hard to think of eleven people that he was that close to.

"I can imagine it would be difficult to round up that many people for the ritual," Astall said, again as if she had read his mind. "And don't worry, I don't think it's something we have to do right now, either."

"Thank goodness for *that*."

"But there is a great deal of wisdom in the *zhian'-tara*. A ceremony of closure, I believe it's referred to.

And closure with Gradak is something you need right now, because his presence could start to interfere with the execution of your duties."

Suddenly apprehensive, Kaz glanced up.

"It's not interfering," he said sharply. "I told you. It's just some bad dreams."

Astall smiled gently. "I said 'could start,' not 'is starting.' If you continue to have nightmares, I think eventually it *will* start interfering. And neither of us wants that to happen. We all have old wounds, Jarem. And that's all right. They ache and linger and become a part of us. And we learn to live with them. But first, we have to make sure they're healed."

"So, what do you propose?"

"I think we need to sit with Gradak for a while and let him tell you about how he lived—and died."

Kaz felt suddenly, strangely uncomfortable. He realized the feeling was vulnerability.

"I have the memories."

"Of course you do. And you know as well as I that unpleasant memories often aren't acknowledged. In traditional therapy, the patient and counselor bring these memories out in a safe place and look at them."

"You sound like you're examining a microbe with the computer," he joked.

"In a way, I am. The brain is the most marvelous computer we've ever known. Nothing, not even Commander Data's positronic brain, has been able to surpass its functioning. Gradak Kaz underwent severe emotional and physical trauma—so severe that it killed him. Those memories need to be seen . . ."

She paused. "No, more than seen. They need to be honored, to be *witnessed,* by Jarem Kaz if he's to make them his own and give Gradak peace."

She spoke quietly, gravely. The weight and seriousness she gave the words sobered him. He looked down at his hands, clasped tightly in his lap.

"I'm not sure I'm ready for that," he said softly.

Astall reached over and gently placed a hand on his knee. "Everything I know tells me that you won't be able to move forward until you do. The closer we get to Cardassian space, the more intense these dreams will become. Gradak wants to be heard."

Kaz looked down at his hands, entwined tightly in his lap. He didn't want to do this. But he knew in his heart that she was right—that things would only get worse instead of better if he didn't address it.

"Then," said Kaz, "I will listen."

Tom Paris was heartily sick of Boreth's library. Hell, he was heartily sick of the entire planet of Boreth.

He felt utterly useless. He couldn't help B'Elanna wade through the seemingly endless piles of scrolls and books. He'd finally figured out how to write with the bone pen, but only just. He had gone through several parchments before he could write anything resembling legible text, and the librarians were not happy with him.

Gura had taken it upon himself to lecture Tom about how difficult it was to make a single piece of parchment.

"First," he had bellowed, "the proper *paagrat* must be culled from the herds. It is fed sacred grains until it is fat enough for our use. Then it is ritually sacrificed when the stars are right. Its skin is scraped and dried and treated to render a single sheet of parchment."

"Sorry," Tom had muttered, thinking that a padd was much more economical and ecologically responsible. Out of some oddly placed sentiment, he'd asked to see one of the animals. Grumbling, Gura had fished out a book and shown him a painting of the beasts.

Tom stared at it for a while. Then, plopping down the open book in front of B'Elanna, he said, "Look at what they use for paper on Boreth."

Her eyes widened and a hand went to her mouth to cover a smile. Softly, so as not to be overheard by the librarians, she muttered, "Oh my God, it's so cute!"

Klingon creatures were usually, to Tom's eyes, as fierce and bristly as Klingons themselves, but *paagrats* were the exception. Looking like miniature gazelles, they had great big eyes and soft, fluffy fur.

"I feel terrible," Tom said. "I'm *writing* on this little guy."

"You've been eating it, too," she said. "We've had it here a couple of times. It's considered a delicacy."

She returned to her research without another blink while Tom stared at the picture of the cute little fellow.

It seemed to stare mournfully back.

"It's enough to make you want to go vegetarian," he said.

"*Tom*," she said, her tone a warning.

"Sorry, it's just . . . We're finding nothing."

She looked up at him. "Which is pretty much what I predicted we'd find. How's that for prophesying?"

Tom shook his head. "I still can't help but believe that there's something there. This is just far too clumsy and archaic a method for anyone to do anything resembling proper research."

He closed the book, unwilling to meet the illustrated *paagrat*'s big-eyed, accusing gaze any longer. "I can't help you, I can't write with this stupid thing, and I'm starting to have doubts about the ethics of scribbling on the skins of really cute little animals."

Her eyes blazed for a moment, then she softened.

"I know. This is pretty frustrating, isn't it?"

" 'Frustrating' is far too nice a word, but I don't want to say what I really think in front of the *paagrat*," he said, pointing to the parchment.

"It's not just the research, is it?"

He met her gaze. There was no lying to her. Softly he said, "For a Klingon, you're a pretty good empath."

"For a Klingon, I'm a pretty good wife," she replied. She regarded him intently. "I'm sorry I asked you to come here. This is my calling, not yours."

He covered her hand with his own. "Hey," he said

softly, "I asked you to marry me, remember? For better or for worse and all that. I'm more than happy to be here, to be with my wife and child."

"I know you mean that, and I love you for it." She squeezed his hand. "But you're miserable and you won't admit it. You don't belong here. I just—I just don't know what to do about it."

If only I'd gotten that first officer position with Chakotay, Tom thought. It had been a bitter blow to him and to B'Elanna when Starfleet's "permission denied" message had come through. He'd fumed at the injustice even as he understood the reasoning. Sure, they didn't want former Maquis in the positions of both captain and first officer.

But damn it, how many times was he going to have to prove himself?

Tom straightened and took a deep breath. He squeezed B'Elanna's hand one last time and then picked up the pen.

"Well, I'm here now, and the least I can do is overcome my squeamishness and see to it that this poor *paagrat* didn't die in vain. Read me the next thing that has any pertinence."

She looked at him searchingly, then smiled. He grinned back.

Sometimes, a man's gotta do what a man's gotta do, he thought, and began to take dictation.

Another large blot formed on the paper.

"Paris," came a rough voice. "You have a message."

Tom looked up from the rapidly spreading pool of black ink to see Commander Logt hovering over him. "A message?"

"Are you deaf as well as foolish?" growled Logt. "A *message*. From Admiral Janeway."

Chapter
13

"ADMIRAL JANEWAY," said Paris, as he stood in the one room of the monastery that permitted modern technology, "you have absolutely no idea how great it is to see you."

Janeway raised an eyebrow at the comment.

"My, my," she said, smothering a smile. "In that case, I'll have to see to it that you get back to Boreth quite frequently."

His heart leaped. Was she implying . . .

"Admiral, if I may speak freely—I'm dying to know what's going on."

"I've got good news, Tom," she replied. "While I don't have a firm offer of a position for you yet, I can at least take you away from Boreth for a while and introduce you to some people."

Paris smiled. "No offense to the Klingons," he said, "but frankly, anywhere that isn't Boreth would be welcome."

"That bad?"

"It's not bad, it's just—well, there's an awful lot of lava caves and you have to write on really cute little animals. But the babysitter's great." Aware that he was babbling, he adopted a more formal tone. "What is it you need from me, Admiral?"

"Tuvok and I are getting ready to attend a conference on a neutral planet called Vaan. It's only a few light-years from Boreth. We're going to be talking with several representatives from various planets who are considering leaving the Federation."

"Why would anyone want to do that?" Tom was genuinely puzzled.

"The reasons vary," Janeway replied. "But much of it has to do with the aftershocks from the Dominion War. Some governments feel that the Federation's policy is too active. That we're too willing to get involved. Many feel we should be more hands-off, as it were."

Tom opened his mouth, but he realized, as an old saying went, that he would be preaching to the choir. Janeway clearly didn't think it was a good idea for these planets to secede, he knew her well enough to know that she shared his approval of the Federation's willingness to get its hands dirty to protect its members—and even planets that weren't members but needed some help.

"I'm not the quadrant's finest diplomat, ma'am," he pointed out.

She smiled. "You're not as bad as you think. Besides, if it's an area in which you think you're weak, then you should brush up on it. You'll need the skills if you're to be a first officer one of these days."

She grew serious. "You spent several years with me just trying to survive, to make it home. The pressure made you into a diamond in my opinion, but I think it's time we added a little polish. You're first officer material, Thomas Eugene Paris, and I'm going to do everything I can to see you sitting in that chair."

He was surprised to find a lump in his throat. Janeway had taken gambles with him from day one. He remembered when they had first met at the New Zealand penal colony, remembered looking up at her as she regarded him thoughtfully, as if running a diagnostic on him with her gaze. He'd been a prisoner, a traitor, the black sheep of a noble starfaring family, and somehow she'd seen something in him that no one else had.

And she continued to see things that no one else had.

He swallowed, hoping that his eyes didn't seem too bright to her. "Thank you, Admiral."

"Don't thank me yet." The twinkle in her eye was back as she added, "You may find yourself longing for the lava caves of Boreth along about the third formal banquet and the fifteenth speech."

* * *

B'Elanna's heart stopped for a moment, and when it resumed beating it was at an accelerated pace. With a hand that trembled, she rested her gloved finger on the sentence. She had to reread it, make absolutely sure that it really said what she thought it said.

Some words in Klingon, she knew, were open to interpretation. Others were as solid as if they had been physically made of stone. She hoped this one was the former.

Translate it however you want to, B'Elanna, she told herself. *Make it read what you want it to read and then move on.*

But she couldn't. She had to know, even if it meant . . . even so. Trying to control her trembling, she rose and carefully bore the parchment over to Lakuur. He scowled as he saw her approach.

"Lakuur, I require assistance in translating this passage."

He raised a thick eyebrow. "I am surprised you have gone this long without asking," he said.

She ignored the insult and held out the scroll. "The third prophecy," she said. "Can the fourth word be translated as 'traveler' or 'wanderer'?"

As anything else but the word that I think it is? she pleaded silently.

"Foolish mongrel," he said, sighing. There was no venom in the words, just resignation. "Of course it can't be. It is exactly what it says it is." Shaking his head, he returned to his work.

Slowly, B'Elanna returned to her chair. She sank down without thinking, staring at the ancient parchment, wondering. Worrying.

The kiss on the back of her neck made her bolt upright. She turned in her chair and found her husband, who had prudently taken two steps back. "Prudently" because her fist was clenched and ready to strike.

"Hey, you haven't even heard my news yet," Tom protested jokingly.

With an effort, B'Elanna unclenched her fist. "What is it? What did Janeway want?" she asked, hoping her voice sounded steady.

"She wants me to accompany her on a diplomatic mission," he said. B'Elanna had never seen him look so happy at the thought of being on a diplomatic mission before, and it made her realize exactly how miserable he'd been.

"Something about trying to talk some planets out of withdrawing from the Federation," Tom continued. "She says there are a lot of people there it could be useful for me to meet."

"Honey, that's wonderful!" She meant the words, but her stomach clenched just the same at the thought of leaving now, just when it looked like—

"When do you have to leave?"

"Janeway said a ship should be here in a few hours. I better get started packing, and I want some time to say good-bye to you properly." He looked at her meaningfully.

At any other time she would have been the one to drag him into their bed, but now . . . She glanced quickly down at the parchment before she set her teeth and rose.

As she walked down the twisting staircase toward their room, B'Elanna resolved that she wouldn't say anything to Tom until he came back. Her news could wait. And this way, she could make sure.

Could make sure that the scroll she had been examining was genuine.

Could make sure that it had not been one of the ones Kohlar had had access to.

Because in examining a list of the so-called prophecies from the *Kuvah'Magh,* there was a phrase that had chilled her to the bone, a phrase that Lakuur had assured her translated precisely in one way only, and was open to no other interpretation:

I am a Voyager.

Tennis, thought Chakotay. Somehow, it fit.

He couldn't see Ellis all sweaty and bloody in a boxing ring (too messy); couldn't imagine his priggish young first officer white-water rafting (too uncomfortable) or swimming (too much exposed skin) or even riding a horse (too smelly). Almost at once, Chakotay amended that; polo would also suit Ellis.

But tennis seemed to fit the younger man to perfection. Janeway, too, had enjoyed playing tennis, so Chakotay was up on his game. But Janeway played her favorite sport the way she did everything else: with intensity, skill, and gusto. She ran for every shot, lobbed back with everything she had. Sweat flew from her brow, her lungs worked, her muscles tensed. Tennis definitely was a workout with her.

Ellis met Chakotay on the holodeck in traditional clothing that was as spotless as Chakotay had expected it to be. His first officer wore a white, short-sleeved shirt with a collar, white shorts, and white socks with, predictably, the appropriate tennis shoes. The shorts and shirt showed off more musculature than Chakotay had expected. Even as he had the thought, Chakotay realized that he should, indeed, have expected it. Of course Ellis would be in excellent shape. All Starfleet officers were supposed to be, and Ellis would be as by-the-book about that as he was about protocol.

"Shall we just practice, or would you like the crowd?" Ellis asked.

"The crowd?"

Ellis nodded. "Doesn't the court look familiar?"

Chakotay looked around, and suddenly became aware of a profusion of purple and green.

"Is this Wimbledon?"

Ellis smiled, his lips curving up under his regulation-length mustache.

"Precisely," he said. "We can even have strawberries and cream during the break if you'd like. Although," he added, "I always worry about spilling on these white clothes."

Of course you would, Chakotay thought. "I could do without the pressure of performing for an audience."

"As you like, Captain. Shall we volley for the serve?"

Chakotay nodded. Ellis executed a perfect serve and Chakotay easily retrieved it, lobbing it over the net. Moving gracefully, Ellis returned the shot, angling it so that Chakotay had to really run for it. He caught it, and it barely cleared the net. Ellis dove, but missed it.

"Excellent! Admiral Janeway has clearly given you a few tips," Ellis said. A holographic little boy with cherubic features, red cheeks, and black hair hurried onto the court and retrieved the ball. Ellis fished in his pocket for another one, tossing it gently to Chakotay.

"You knew that Janeway was fond of tennis?" Deftly, Chakotay caught the ball.

"Of course," said Ellis. "Priggy does his research, Captain."

Chakotay looked at him sharply but saw only humor. Maybe he did know about the nickname after all and was choosing to join in the joke. Either that, or he had decided to be a good sport after Chakotay had accidentally mentioned it earlier.

Ellis continued, "You like to box, Tom Paris enjoys twentieth-century automobiles, the multitalented Harry Kim plays the clarinet *and* the saxophone, the Doctor is fond of opera, Seven of Nine is a gourmet cook. . . . Shall I go on?"

Chakotay laughed a little. "What about Andrew Ellis?"

"Andrew Ellis enjoys tennis, polo, golf, and, believe it or not, the ancient art of origami."

"Actually," said Chakotay, "that doesn't surprise me at all. Origami is all about precision. Now, if Commander Ellis was a secret fan of finger painting or mud wrestling, that might surprise me. Love all," he said, announcing the score, and served.

Chakotay didn't have the superior form that Ellis displayed, but he put a lot of power into the serve, and for a brief instant the first officer was caught off guard. He rallied, though, diving for the ball with exuberance, and returned it. They lobbied for a while, then Chakotay narrowly missed a shot.

As he picked up the ball and bounced it a few times, Ellis said, apropos of nothing, "I eat raw cookie dough."

Chakotay's head whipped up. Ellis was turning a little pink, and not from exertion.

"What?"

"I eat raw cookie dough," Ellis said, sounding embarrassed. "One isn't supposed to do that, you know. Raw eggs and so forth. But I can't help sneaking a bite of it now and then. A lady friend introduced me to it. It tastes completely different from the end product."

Chakotay stared, then laughed out loud. For Ellis, this was living life on the edge.

"I see that you're a devil-may-care rebel, Mr. Ellis, and I'm going to have to watch you very carefully." Still grinning, Chakotay lifted his racket and announced, "Love serving fifteen."

*   *   *

Sekaya paced in her quarters, deep in thought, wondering what she should do. When her combadge chirped and Astall's voice said, "Counselor Astall to Sekaya," it startled her so that she gasped aloud.

She recovered quickly and said in a calm voice, "Yes, Astall, what is it?"

"I have a patient who's having some bad dreams," Astall said. "I'm going to be doing a counseling session that isolates . . . oh, golly, it's too hard to explain without naming him and he said that was all right."

Sekaya grinned at the Huanni's bubbly voice. "If he gave his permission to discuss the session, then I'm happy to help. Who is it? One of the colonists?"

"No, it's Dr. Kaz."

"Really?"

"His former host was a Maquis who was killed at Tevlik's moon, and this host is stirring now that we're entering former Cardassian space."

Suddenly, Sekaya felt cold. For a defeated race, the Cardassians continued to hound their victims with shocking perseverance. She rubbed her upper arms and reached for a blanket.

"Go on."

"I wanted to get your advice on the session I plan to conduct with him," Astall continued. "It's actually a lot like a ritual, and I thought you might have some insight."

Sekaya listened intently, occasionally making a

comment or a recommendation, as Astall filled her in. The Huanni was right: the session did have a lot in common with a ritual. "Sounds almost like a spirit walk," Sekaya said.

"A what?"

"A spirit walk. Where we enter an altered state of mind and converse with people or beings on a spiritual plane."

"The active imagination technique espoused by Carl Jung!" said Astall. Her excitement came through clearly. Sekaya wondered if the counselor might actually be jumping up and down.

"Yes, exactly."

"I like your term."

"So do we." Sekaya realized she was smiling. "Use it if you like. Would you like me to assist you?"

"I don't think that will be necessary. Kaz seems to be more comfortable with scientific rather than spiritual treatments."

Sekaya thought about what she knew of the handsome doctor and had to agree. "I think you're right. If you change your mind, I would be honored to assist you."

"You're sweet to offer! Astall out."

Although the conversation had been on an entirely different topic than the one Sekaya had been brooding on earlier, it had helped her clear her mind.

"Computer, locate Captain Chakotay," she said.

"Captain Chakotay is in Holodeck One."

"Is he alone?"

"Commander Andrew Ellis is also in Holodeck One."

"Damn," Sekaya muttered, her newfound resolve crumbling. She wanted very badly to finish the conversation she and her brother had started the other night over dinner, but didn't want to interrupt anything. Sekaya loved Chakotay and hated lying to him. At the time, she knew she hadn't been up to the difficult task. Now, though, her instincts were telling her that bringing him into the loop was the right thing to do, and who knew when she'd have a better chance.

Or was it really the right thing to do? She tugged on her long hair, which at the moment she wore in a braid. It was a nervous habit left over from childhood that only emerged in times of great stress. Should she tell him now, or later? Tell him everything, or just give him the general picture?

She was second-guessing herself. Sekaya could help others make clear, compassionate decisions, but now, she felt torn in so many directions she couldn't see the right path.

But she didn't need to make this decision alone. She could ask for help.

Calmed by the thought, Sekaya retrieved her medicine bundle from where she had tucked it in one of the drawers. She sat down cross-legged on the floor and reverently unfolded the fabric.

Each individual's medicine bundle was unique. It reflected what they had "seen" during vision quests, or stumbled upon, or received as a gift for whatever reasons. Medicine bundles were also rather private. One was not forbidden to share the contents with another during ritual moments, but sharing was a gesture of great trust and affection. Sekaya recalled being surprised when Chakotay revealed to her that he had shared his medicine bundle with Janeway, and wondered a bit about the motivation behind that. Despite his more recent involvement with the Borg woman, Seven of Nine, Sekaya suspected that her brother just might be carrying a bit of a torch for his former captain.

Her own bundle contained an *akoonah,* the shed skin of a snake, a fragment of an antler tine, a stone from a lake, similar to one her brother had, and a small tree branch upon which she had carved traditional symbols.

She took a few long, slow breaths to calm herself, and then placed her hand on the *akoonah.* It felt warm and tingly, and she closed her eyes and opened her soul to the familiar, comforting sensation.

"We are far from the sacred places of our grandfathers," she whispered. "We are far from the bones of our people. I come here seeking guidance."

She opened her eyes and found herself standing in a lush forest. Above her, bright sunlight filtered through the feathery branches of evergreen trees, making dancing patches on the needle-strewn forest floor. She knew this place; knew who dwelt here. Sekaya stood barefoot on the loam, sinking her toes into the richly scented earth, the pine needles pliable and softened with rain. She breathed deeply of the pine scent, and heard a soft sound behind her.

He had come, as she hoped He would. She never knew who would come to her call, as the spirits decided among themselves which of Them was best suited to a supplicant's particular need. Even so, there were some animal spirits that were particularly fond of their chosen human, and came more frequently than others.

Stag was such a spirit for Sekaya. He was a mighty white-tailed buck, with large, liquid brown eyes and an enormous rack. On a visit to Earth, she had felt drawn to a discarded antler tine, and had added it to her medicine bundle. He had chosen her. Stag had been coming to her ever since.

Sekaya walked toward Him now, her heart welling with affection. She permitted all the emotions she was holding to come to the surface: fear, worry, grief, delight. He would take and sanctify them all. Gently she stroked His soft neck, feeling the warmth of His short fur and the strength of His muscles. He brushed her cheek with His soft, moist nose.

"Daughter of the Forest," He said gently, using her spirit name. "Your heart is troubled. What can I do to ease your pain?"

Sekaya had heard that spirit guides often practiced a form of "tough love." But Stag had always been so gentle and tender with her. Responding immediately to that tenderness, Sekaya felt tears welling in her eyes.

"*I am torn between keeping a secret of my people and sharing it with my brother,*" she whispered. The tears flowed down her cheeks now. Gently, Stag licked them away with His warm tongue.

"*Is not your brother of your people?*" He asked.

"*Yes,*" she admitted, "*but he turned away from our teachings a long time ago. He only returned to them out of pain and duty.*"

He looked at her lovingly. "*Would it comfort you to know that We are aware of Chakotay? That We have been with him often?*"

"*Yes,*" Sekaya replied. "*It would surprise me, but it would comfort me.*"

"*Then, Daughter, be both surprised and comforted,*" Stag said, amused. "*Chakotay is more like you than you would think.*"

"*Then . . . you think I should tell him?*"

"*I will say to you exactly what you knew I would say,*" Stag replied maddeningly. "*You need to weigh the need to keep the secret with Chakotay's need to know. Until he understands what your people went through at the hands of the Cardassians, he can never truly belong to you.*"

She sank down onto the forest floor. He knelt beside her and placed His mighty head in her lap, like a unicorn out of the old tales. He was careful to avoid harming her with His sharp tines.

"*I want him to belong with us,*" Sekaya said. She stroked His neck, touched His long, velvety soft ears *and ran their length through her fingers. "But I do not wish to relive that pain."*

"You must decide," said Stag. "But I can tell you this: He is being groomed for a great destiny, and one who has a great destiny needs a great heart full of compassion."

"Like yours," Sekaya whispered fondly.

"Like yours," came another voice. And before she realized what was happening, Sekaya realized that she no longer cradled Stag's mighty head in her lap, but that of a boy about seven years old. A boy who was familiar to her.

Commingled pain and delight rose in her heart. When they had been reunited six months ago, Chakotay had told his sister he had spirit-walked with their father when he was attuned with the akoonah. *Sekaya herself had never seen her father when she was deep in meditation in the spirit world. She suspected that it was because she and her father had had no rift in life. She grieved Kolopak's passing as any daughter would, especially coming the way it had, but felt no need to embark on a spirit walk with him.*

But this boy . . .

His face was tranquil as he smiled up at her, as calm and untroubled as the surface of a lake on a clear day. That was why he had been given his name: Blue Water Boy. A lake needed to be calm before it could hold the reflection of the sky, he had told her once; before it could rightly be said to be "blue water."

She did not want to see him. Sekaya felt fear, panic, and guilt rise inside her. She scooted backward and scrambled to her feet, aware that suddenly she, too, was only six years old. She looked up from where Blue Water Boy sat, brushing pine needles out of his long, thick hair, and into the dark eyes of her brother.

The two boys, friends almost since birth, had never seemed a logical pair. Whereas Blue Water Boy was almost unnaturally calm, Chakotay always seemed to Sekaya to be like a caged beast. He never wanted to be where he was at any given time; he always wanted to do something different. But she loved both of these boys so much, and they loved one another. If Blue Water Boy had been of her own tribe, Sekaya thought that her parents would have made him an honorary son-brother. But Blue Water Boy was Oglala Lakota, and friendship was the closest bond they would be allowed to share.

Both the young Chakotay and the Lakota boy were looking directly at her now, Chakotay with his almost quivering brand of intensity and Blue Water Boy with his still, deep, unnerving regard. Blue Water Boy got to his feet and opened his hands. Nestled in each palm was a small, round stone, polished to a glassy smoothness by centuries of immersion in water.

"These are for you," he said. "I dove deep and found them. Chakotay, this one is from the river. I thought it would suit you. The river is rushing and wild and fast. Always in a hurry to get somewhere."

The young Chakotay grinned a little sheepishly and took the stone.

"Thank you," he said. "I will put it in my medicine bundle when I am older."

Blue Water Boy now turned to Sekaya. "This one," he said, "is also a gift from the water, but it's from the lake." His eyes bore into hers with a solemnity far beyond his years, and inside, where she was an adult, Sekaya shivered.

Her heart ached for him, but she thought she knew why he had appeared to her today. He had given her and Chakotay a gift. Now, it was time for her to give something to Chakotay. She made her decision. Sekaya took a deep breath and opened her eyes.

She saw again the attractive but neutral décor of her quarters, and gazed once more at the contents of her medicine bundle. Her right hand still tingled from the contact with the *akoonah*, but not unpleasantly.

Her left hand clutched the lake stone Blue Water Boy had given her over thirty years ago.

Her eyes were wet. She wiped at her face. She refolded the bundle, gently returning the stone and the *akoonah* to it, said a little prayer of thanks for the vision it had granted her, and returned it to safekeeping in the drawer.

"Computer," she said, realizing how thick her voice sounded, "are Captain Chakotay and Commander Ellis still in Holodeck One?"

"Affirmative."

She sighed. *Well,* she thought, *better to interrupt him at his play than at his work.* They would shortly arrive at the colony, and then he would have other things to think about.

Sekaya took a deep breath and headed for the turbolift.

Chapter

14

ON ASTALL'S ADVICE, Kaz returned to his quarters for a shower. *Deliberately preparing for something often eases one into a certain accepting state of mind,* she had told him. He finished the shower and changed into a fresh uniform, his thoughts racing. Kaz thought he would much rather have simply started right in on whatever it was the counselor had in mind. Having time to think about it served only to increase his apprehension.

Still, the Huanni was the expert here, and he wouldn't have liked her telling him how to go about treating a broken leg, so he obliged. He returned to her quarters about a half-hour later.

She smiled at him as he entered. "Perfect timing. I've just finished getting ready."

Kaz noticed the lights were dimmer than they were earlier, and there was a pleasant smell in the air. He sniffed, trying to identify it.

"It's lavender," Astall explained. "It's an herb traditionally used on Earth for its calming effect. I can eliminate it if it's unpleasant."

"No, no, it's fine. I like it," Kaz said. The scent was clean and slightly sweet. He didn't know about its calming him, though. He sat and looked up at her expectantly.

Astall handed him a cup of a steaming beverage. "Chamomile tea," she said. "Also known for its calming effect. And it's pretty tasty as well. Have a few sips and I'll explain what we'll be doing."

She glanced at the chronometer. "I checked with Lieutenant Kim. It's going to be another several days before we arrive at Loran II at this speed, and that should be plenty of time for us to complete the process and for you to reflect on it and integrate it."

Kaz tried not to look as nervous as he felt, but he suspected the rattling of the delicate china cup in its saucer gave him away.

"I've studied nearly every therapy technique practiced by humanoids within the Federation," Astall continued. "What we're going to do now is a combination of guided meditation, hypnotherapy, and a greatly simplified version of the *zhian'tara*. I won't be using any medication at all. We want your mind clear."

"All right." Kaz nodded and sipped the tea. Astall was right: it was good.

"We're going to address the memories of Gradak that are contained in the Kaz symbiont. We're going to ask him to step into your body—in a purely symbolic way, of course—and let him tell us exactly what it is that's bothering him so badly. Once he has told us this, we'll ask him to return to the symbiont and take his place with the memories of all the other hosts that have gone before."

Kaz stared into the depths of his cup. "What if he doesn't want to leave?"

Astall smiled gently. "As I said, this is symbolic, not literal. He will never really be present, so that's not an issue. This is all about accessing memory, Jarem, not channeling a dead spirit. That sort of thing is more Sekaya's job."

Kaz's eyebrows shot upward. "Sekaya can do that?"

"I'm not sure, but certainly she'd be better equipped to handle anything like that than I would!" Astall said. "Let's see if I can put it another way. You understand about the workings of the humanoid brain. It varies from species to species, of course—heck, it varies from person to person and even brain hemisphere to hemisphere—but there are more similarities than differences. Memories, both long- and short-term, are stored in the medial temporal lobe, specifically, in the hippocampus. And correct me if I've got this wrong, but the Trill neural transmitter isoboromine is what connects the memories contained in the symbiont to the brain of the current host."

"That's more or less right," Jarem said, smiling.

"As long as I've got the gist of it. We're simply turning things around a bit. Right now, you have access to the memories of all the symbiont's previous hosts along with Jarem's. At the present moment, Jarem's memories are in the forefront. Which is as it should be as you are the current, living host."

She held out her left hand, relaxed and open, to try to illustrate the point.

"Gradak's are more deeply embedded, less immediate." Astall closed her right hand into a loose fist and held it close to her heart. "We're going to bring Gradak's memories into that center-stage position while Jarem's step back a little. That's all."

As she spoke, she shifted position with her hands, bringing the left hand to her heart and extending and opening the right. It was a graceful and fluid gesture, and Jarem grasped exactly what she planned to do. He nodded his understanding. He felt much better now that she had explained it in a somewhat more dispassionate, scientific way.

"Got it."

"Then, when we're done, we'll shift things back to their proper places. You won't lose any memories; you'll just feel Gradak's as more immediate for a while."

"Any side effects?" he joked.

"I think it likely that you might feel a bit unsettled afterward," she said. "It will take some time for you to readjust to being Jarem Kaz and not Gradak Kaz. Fortunately, we're not due to arrive at Loran II for another few days, so we do have that time. And we both expect that some of his memories that will surface could be traumatic, and you'll have to deal with that. But that's about it."

A thought struck Kaz. "Have you done this before?"

"Not with a Trill," she said. "I've done this sort of guided meditation quite often, though."

She leaned forward and looked at him intently. "Jarem, we don't have to do this. We can wait until we return from this mission, and then you can take some leave and visit Trill. I'm sure they'd be better equipped to handle this than I would. If you have any reservations about the process I've outlined, I'll certainly understand. This has to be your decision—Jarem's decision."

Kaz thought about it. He appreciated Astall's frankness, but what she was proposing didn't sound dangerous. He was familiar with the techniques she mentioned. While their efficacy could not be proved conclusively in a lab, he knew that sometimes it was very helpful and had never heard of any ill effects.

He thought of the recurring nightmare, of the screams and the blood and the fire, of Gradak's pain and rage, and couldn't suppress a shudder. If this helped quash the nightmares, it was more than worth the minimal risk.

"Let's do it."

At her gesture, he moved to the sofa and stretched out. She put a blanket over him and he smiled wryly. "Do you provide teddy bears too?"

Her eyes danced. "Indeed I do, would you like one?"

He chuckled. "I'm not taking a nap."

"No, but body temperature often drops during times of deep relaxation," Astall said. "I just want to make sure you are completely comfortable. Now, close your eyes."

Feeling a little self-conscious, Kaz did so.

"Comfy?"

"Very."

"Good. Now, take a long, slow, deep breath through your nose and let it out through your mouth."

He inhaled the fresh scent of lavender with each breath and felt himself relaxing.

"Again." Kaz repeated the breathing exercise several more times. After a while, he noticed that he felt very calm, but not sleepy.

Astall's voice drifted to him. "Jarem, I want you to imagine yourself in a place that makes you feel very peaceful. Take your time and make all the details vivid. When you can see it in your mind's eye, let me know."

It was easier than he expected to visualize himself back on his homeworld, walking by the ocean and gazing out into its purple depths. The rhythm of the waves was soothing.

"I'm there," he said. It was hard to move his lips to speak.

"Good. Now, I want you to imagine Gradak standing

right beside you. And I want you to visualize him being calm and at peace as well."

Jarem felt himself tense a little. In the deep place of imagination, he turned his head and saw Gradak.

He was not calm and at peace.

He wore torn, burned, bloodstained clothing, and the wounds that would eventually bring his death cried out to Jarem as silently and as forcefully as Gradak's unheard words.

Sitting in the captain's chair where he had spent so many night shifts during the past seven years, Kim gazed absently at the viewscreen. The stars streaked past as *Voyager* continued its uneventful journey.

He checked the chronometer to discover that Chakotay had exceeded his time in the holodeck with Ellis by about two minutes. Kim debated notifying his commanding officer, as it was time to drop down to warp two for the rest of the journey. Sekaya had suggested that they extend the trip, as she wanted to have more time to talk with the colonists. Traveling at warp two would take them about three more days to reach Loran II; if they continued at the present speed, they'd arrive in a few hours.

He decided to execute the order himself. It wasn't as if it was a particularly demanding one, and if Chakotay was actually having a good time with his prickly first officer, Kim didn't want to interrupt.

"Lieutenant Tare," Kim said, "drop to warp two."

"Aye, sir."

"Lieutenant Campbell, engage long-range scanners. Report anything unusual."

Campbell, standing at his old station, frowned. "Sir, I'm picking up signs of debris on the long-range scanners."

"Lieutenant Tare, drop out of warp," Kim ordered, instantly alert.

"Aye, sir." The new pilot executed the order every bit as smoothly as Tom Paris could have done. Kim stared now at open space.

"The debris is approximately eighteen million kilometers ahead," Campbell said.

"Magnify," Kim said.

His eyes widened, ever so slightly, at what he saw.

Ka-thok. Chakotay grunted as he returned the shot, doing his utmost to put spin on the ball. Ellis dove for it easily and sent it back over the net. Damn him, the man wasn't even breaking a sweat!

Chakotay ran for the ball, bringing his racket across his body for a good solid backhand.

"Captain Chakotay, please report to the bridge."

Chakotay stumbled in midstride and missed the ball. Gasping for breath, he drew a hand over his forehead, grateful for the sweatbands on his wrists. He tapped his combadge.

"What's going on, Harry?"

"Captain, there's something here you should see."

"We're on our way." Chakotay and his first officer exchanged glances as they left the holodeck.

Still clad in their tennis whites, they emerged on the bridge. The instant he glanced up at the viewscreen, Chakotay realized exactly why Harry had wanted him to see this.

On the long-range sensors was the wreckage of dozens of vessels.

Gradak was older than Jarem, but still in the prime of life. Slender, gray-haired, hollow-cheeked, he was talking rapidly; his mouth was moving, but Jarem heard nothing. The other Trill's eyes were wild and bloodshot, and he punctuated his unheard speech with agitated gestures.

"Describe him to me," asked Astall.

"He's very upset," Kaz said aloud. "Very angry. He's wounded and bloody, and he's shouting things at me, but I can't hear him."

"Jarem, this is your body," Astall said. Her voice was calm, soothing. "You are in control of it at all times. I want you to imagine your memories as something physical, something you can hold in your hand."

In his mind, Jarem looked down at his left hand. Cradled in his palm was a stone. It seemed to radiate and pulse, as if something was contained within it, and it changed colors as Jarem watched. Intellectually, he wondered at the image. He had certainly never thought of his memories as looking quite like that.

"I see them," he said, amending at once, "It. The—the memory stone."

"Now, look at Gradak. Does he have his memories in his hand too?"

Kaz didn't want to look at Gradak, but he forced himself to do so. The blood-covered Trill seemed slightly less frantic. He, too, had a beautiful, radiant "stone" in his left hand. He held it out to Jarem, his weathered face imploring.

"Yes," said Jarem. "He has his memories. He wants me to take them."

"That's exactly what you should do. Give him your memories, and take his."

But Kaz couldn't do it. He was afraid of having this man's memories be uppermost in his mind. Jarem didn't have to relive Gradak's life—and death—in order to sense his outrage, grief, and burning need for revenge. They were written plainly on the dead man's face. Gradak continued to hold out his hands, one holding his own memories, the other empty, ready to take Jarem's memories.

"I don't want them," Kaz whispered.

"He will give them to you whether you want them or not," came Astall's voice. "He had been doing everything he can to give them to you through your dreams. If you willingly take on these memories, you will be in control. Otherwise, Gradak will be running the show, and he's in too much pain to be doing that."

Gradak was speaking again, or trying to; Jarem still

couldn't hear him. The Maquis gesticulated with the hand that held the memories.

Slowly, reluctantly, Jarem extended his hands. He saw that they trembled as his right hand closed over Gradak's memory stone. His left hand felt oddly empty as Gradak folded his bloodstained hands around the stone and lifted Jarem's memories.

Kaz's eyes flew open.

The memories crashed upon him like a tidal wave. They came so swiftly, so powerfully, he had trouble breathing.

Vallia. In his arms again, her sweat-slicked skin against his, her mouth open to him, sweet—

Taken. Rounded up like beasts by the Cardassian monsters. Taken to who knew where. "You can leave. We only want the Bajorans." And so, broken and weeping, he left, rather than throw his life away in a futile attempt to find her; left only to return, to kill as many Cardassians as he could—

"Jarem. . . ?"

Safe here, on Tevlik's moon. Brought here by the one man he really trusted—Arak Katal. The starlight caught Katal's earring, making it glitter. Glitter like his eyes, burning with passion to free his people. Side by side they fought. Friends. Brothers in arms.

"Traitor!" cried Kaz, surging upward. *"Murderer!"*

There was a warm hand on his. Gradak/Jarem knew that he was safe aboard *Voyager,* in Astall's quarters. The Huanni knew what she was doing, and he trusted her. The hand was a lifeline, solid and reassuring. He clutched it hard, feeling the long, thin, delicate bones of her fingers give beneath the pressure. In a distant part of his mind, he knew he was hurting her. But she didn't let go.

"Gradak Kaz," Astall said, "your memories are in the forefront now. Jarem has given you the space to speak."

Jarem felt Gradak's pain and hope. The need to speak, to share his pain, to let this kind female know what had happened to him, to Vallia, to the thousands on Tevlik's moon. He looked at her with eyes that both saw and did not see, and opened his mouth.

For an instant, the sound was familiar and alien at the same time. Then Kaz realized what it was: the noise of his combadge.

"Chakotay to Dr. Kaz and Commander Astall. Report to the bridge at once."

Chapter
15

KAZ CLUTCHED Astall's hands so hard he feared he
would snap the bones.

"No," he gasped. "Listen to me. *Listen!* I have to tell
you—"

Astall squeezed his hands and then disengaged herself from their grip.

"Take slow, deep breaths," she said softly. "I'll be
back in a moment."

He heard her talking in a quiet voice, heard Chakotay answer, but didn't give a damn about the words. Inside, Gradak's memories, raw and seething like a lava
pit, were demanding acknowledgment.

Again, Kaz felt the light touch of the Huanni's hand,
this time gently stroking his forehead.

"It's important," she said softly. "Captain Chakotay wants to see both of us on the bridge. I'm so sorry, but we'll have to finish this at a later time."

"Later?" There was nothing of Jarem in the vitriolic tone of voice. This was Gradak, in agony, outraged at again being ignored and pushed aside.

"Gradak," said Astall, her voice completely unruffled by the outburst, "You will be heard. I swear this to you. But the body in which your memories dwell has a duty to his people, just as you did to yours. He's needed now. You will not interfere with him."

"He understands," said Jarem, his voice hoarse from the screams. "But he's not going back to where he was. Not until he's damn good and ready."

"I'm not surprised," said Astall. There was a hint of admiration in her voice. "Gradak was clearly a very strong individual. Now, Jarem Kaz. Take another deep breath. See yourself settling back firmly into your body, and then open your eyes."

He did as she told him, and it was a relief to look down at his body and see it whole and without bloodstains. He realized he was trembling.

She helped him sit up. "How do you feel?" she asked, her big purple eyes full of concern as she stroked his hair gently.

"Okay," he said, lying a little. His heart was racing.

She searched his face. "Jarem, if you like, I can relieve you of duty for a few hours. We can go ahead and finish this."

He grimaced. "Absolutely not," he said. "This is the first time the captain has asked for me, and I'm not going to put him off."

Her ears flapped gently, revealing her concern even more clearly than her expression did.

"I don't like the thought of you running around with Gradak so intensely active in your head."

"He's always been in my head, as have the others."

"Not like this."

"No," Kaz was forced to agree, "not like this. But I can manage."

"If you have any suspicions that you can't," she said, "I want you back here immediately. Is that understood?"

Kaz had to grin. "Aye, ma'am. Come on. We need to get to the bridge and find out what's going on."

Sekaya reached the holodeck and stared at the closed doors. She took a deep, steadying breath.

"Computer, open door to Holodeck One."

The door opened. Sekaya was puzzled when she peered into the holodeck and saw only an empty room that looked rather like a cargo bay.

"Computer," she asked, "Where is Captain Chakotay?"

"Captain Chakotay is on the bridge."

Sekaya made a noise of exasperation. She didn't want to bring up the subject there, in front of everyone, but perhaps she could arrange a time to discuss it with him. She headed for the turbolift.

When she appeared on the bridge and glanced casually at the screen, she gasped. The sound was soft, but Chakotay had excellent hearing. He turned to look at her.

"Good timing, Sekaya. I was just about to ask you to come up," he said. "Kaz, Astall, and Fortier are on their way as well."

As if mesmerized, Sekaya walked slowly down to the screen. She hadn't spent a lot of time in space, and the glimpses into the stars still enchanted her. But what she was regarding now, she knew, was not of the stars and space. These were the things of men.

"What is all of this?" she asked. "How close are we to Loran II?"

"It's debris from various sources," said Kim, answering the first question but not the second. The turbolift door hissed open. Fortier, Astall, and Kaz emerged.

Like Sekaya, Fortier gasped at the sight. *"Mon dieu,"* he said softly.

"The wreckage isn't recent," Ellis said, forestalling the question. "It looks like there was a battle here some time ago."

"These were Federation and Cardassian ships," said Kim.

"I was not aware there were any battles fought in this area of space," said Fortier. His voice was admirably calm, but Sekaya could see that his hands trembled slightly. "How close are we to Loran II?" he asked, echoing Sekaya.

"Not that far. I'd planned to slow down at this point, take our time getting there," said Chakotay. "But given this," he added, indicating the debris, "I'm inclined to continue at our present speed. You were right, Mr. Fortier. We have no records of any battles being fought here, but obviously, we can see that that doesn't mean it didn't happen."

"None of these was a particularly big ship," said Kim, his eyes on the controls. "I'm picking up readings of Cardassian shuttles and freighters as well as the wreckage of a few Federation shuttles, three Maquis fighters, and one *Peregrine*-class courier."

"Also known as a Maquis interceptor," said Chakotay.

"A skirmish, then," said Kaz, looking intently at the floating ruins on the screen. "Not a battle. And probably between Maquis and Cardassians. I'll bet anything those Federation ships were stolen."

Sekaya glanced at him. His voice sounded deeper, slightly harsher, and he carried himself a little differently. She recalled that Astall had told her that one of his hosts had been a Maquis. Maybe he was remembering his time in the fight. Or maybe she was just imagining it; she had, after all, met Kaz for only a few brief moments.

"The doctor's right," Kim said. "I'm confirming the identities of some of the vessels, and they were reported stolen by the Maquis several years ago."

Chakotay, like Kaz, had tensed slightly. "That's good news," he said. "If it was a small skirmish, it's less likely to have affected Fortier's colony. Also, we should keep in mind that this debris could have been drifting for some time. The battle could have occurred nowhere near Loran II."

"On the negative side," said Ellis, "depending of course on the amount of drift, a Class-M planet in the area wouldn't go unnoticed, especially if anyone had to make an emergency landing for repairs."

Sekaya winced inwardly. Chakotay had been trying to cast a positive spin on an alarming situation, but this first officer of his didn't seem to realize how deeply it affected *Voyager*'s passengers. Loran II wasn't just another Class-M planet; it was home to these people. It was where their loved ones were—or so everyone hoped.

"Lieutenant Tare," said Chakotay, ignoring Ellis, "how far does the debris field extend, and is it possible for us to get through it?"

Tare's dark hands moved with expertise over the controls. "It's pretty extensive, sir," she said. "There's scattered debris more or less all the way to Loran II. It may not have been a full-blown battle, but this was obviously a hot area of space for a while. I can plot a path, however, that steers clear of it."

"How tricky will navigating it be? Will we be able to go to warp?"

Tare scrutinized the data. "We can go to warp," she decided.

Fortier swallowed hard. Astall moved to step beside the colonist leader and put a reassuring hand on his shoulder. Sekaya, too, knew what the man was thinking: *Did this reach my land? Did this war claim my people?*

"Then resume course, Lieutenant. Warp nine." Chakotay looked at his guest. "Mr. Fortier, you are, of course, welcome to stay on the bridge, or you may wish to take this time to notify and prepare your people."

Fortier looked at Chakotay appraisingly. There was no real need to hurry, and he knew it. The debris was old. The colonists who had remained on Loran II had said nothing of an attack, and it was only recently that they had ceased to be heard from.

But Sekaya knew her brother, and knew that he was concerned about the colonists. Now that there was a reason to be concerned, even an old reason, Chakotay was going to see to it that the colonists learned as soon as possible the fate of their friends who had remained behind. And Fortier recognized what Chakotay had done for him.

"Thank you, Captain. I think I will tell my companions. They . . . will want to know. I appreciate your willingness to hasten our arrival."

"Of course."

Astall stopped Fortier on his way out, placing a gentle hand on his arm.

"Please let me know if Sekaya and I can be of any help," she said earnestly.

Fortier's face softened, and Sekaya wondered if those were tears in his eyes. Huanni often tended to bring out the best in people, she had observed. They encouraged people to be soft, to be open, when it was so easy, so natural, to be hard and defensive.

"Thank you," Fortier replied gently, then left.

Sekaya turned toward her brother and regarded him. Quietly, he said, "Sekaya, you came to the bridge before I requested your presence. Did you . . . need to see me about anything?"

Yes, she cried inwardly. *I need to tell you what happened to us. I need to let you know what they did.*

She cleared her throat. "Yes, but it can wait. The Loran II situation needs our immediate attention." She hesitated, then said, "On the way back, we'll talk, yes?"

He smiled, the smile she remembered from their childhood, the smile that had always warmed her heart.

"Of course. I look forward to it."

Kaz was aware that his heart was beating rapidly. Sweat gathered at his hairline, and he clenched his fists. Seeing the ruins of old Maquis ships, the type of ship that he himself had flown, knowing that his friends had died here—

No, damn it, he thought. *I never flew a Maquis fighter. I knew no Maquis personally until after the war. These are Gradak's feelings, not mine.*

Astall stood beside him in the turbolift. They were alone. For a while, they didn't speak, but he was fully aware that the Huanni was keenly observing his every reaction, every expression that flitted across the face he was trying so hard to keep impassive.

"We still have a few hours until we reach Loran II," she said at last. "There would be time for us to finish what we started."

He looked at her then. "Can you guarantee that there won't be any lingering effects that might impair my performance as a physician?"

Astall sighed. "No. There's no question that it will be emotionally intense. Ideally, I'd want to have a buffer zone to factor in recovery time."

Kaz shrugged and sighed. "We've just found one thing we didn't expect out here—wreckage from a battle we didn't even know had been fought. We might very well find something else. I have to be at full capacity in case there are injured who need immediate treatment."

She regarded him steadily. "Gradak is still very much present with you. Are you at full capacity right now?"

Silently, Kaz asked himself that question. The answer was a definite yes. Unhappy as Gradak was, his memories prowling around in Kaz's brain like a caged animal, Kaz knew the Maquis would not stand in the way of anything Jarem Kaz needed to do in his capacity as a doctor. Gradak knew full well how awful it was to lose a loved one. He'd stay at bay rather than interfere with Kaz's duties.

At least, for now.

But if Gradak Kaz were allowed to speak, what kind of reaction would Jarem Kaz have? How exhausted or depleted would he be by the experience?

What kind of mistakes does a distracted doctor make?

"Yes," Kaz said. "I'm fully competent."

Astall sighed. Her ears drooped slightly. "I'm sorry. I suppose I should have waited."

"We couldn't have known we'd come across a battlefield," said Kaz. "And I completely agreed with you. I wanted to have this over and done with too."

"Well, let's just hope that we won't encounter anything too unusual on Loran II. We can drop off the colonists and get on our way. Then we can give Gradak the audience he's waited for so patiently."

Kaz couldn't think of anything he'd like better.

Chakotay quickly changed out of his tennis clothing and back into his uniform. When he returned to the bridge, he saw that Ellis had done the same.

"We'll finish the game up later," he told his first officer as he sat in the command chair and called up his computer.

Long-range sensors were pulling in vast amounts of data, but there seemed to be nothing significant yet. The debris they had encountered did not overly trouble Chakotay. The war had been a long and bitter one. It was likely that Federation starships would keep stumbling across unknown battlefields like this one for many years to come.

Nor did Ellis's badly timed, dispassionate comment about M-Class worlds bother him. But he knew that Fortier was worried, and so he had increased *Voyager*'s speed. The sooner they got to Loran II and discovered what remained there, the better Chakotay would like it, whether it was good news or bad.

Sekaya's door chimed softly. "Come," she called.

The door hissed open and Fortier entered. She welcomed him with a smile and waved him in. She was sitting on the floor. In front of her she had spread an assortment of various representational items.

"I'm pleased you decided to come," she said. "How are your people handling the news?"

He shrugged as he sat beside her. "They took it well enough. I tried to concentrate on what Captain Chakotay had said, to emphasize that the battle had been fought some time ago and we had been in communication with our families on the planet until very recently. But one can't help but worry."

Sekaya nodded sympathetically. "I understand," she said. "And so does my brother. At least we'll be there in just a few hours."

"Your brother?" His eyes traveled over her face and then his lips curved into a smile and he nodded. "Ah, yes, I see the resemblance now. You are very similar, in fact. You're not twins, are you?"

She smiled. "No. Chakotay's a little older than I am, but we are very much alike."

He nodded. "Indeed. So, Sekaya—you asked me to come. I am here. What is it you wish?"

"I wanted to know if you had given any thought to

what we discussed in the holodeck—about doing a ritual."

His expression darkened. "I don't know what kind of ritual to prepare. I don't know what we're going to find."

Gently, Sekaya said, "I thought of that. I have two ideas I'd like to discuss with you. One would be a sort of offering to the land. It would thank the planet for taking care of your people and welcoming them back to stay. The second one would be . . . would be to honor the dead."

He regarded her steadily. "You think we will find our families dead, then?"

She met his gaze without flinching. "I don't know any more than you do. But it's a possibility. You are too intelligent a man not to know that."

Fortier smiled sadly. "Intelligent, perhaps. Hopeful, certainly. But you are right. We should prepare both ceremonies, just in case."

Sekaya gestured to the objects spread before her. "These are items typical of what I might use if I were designing the ritual for my people. These symbols all have meaning; the items represent the elements and some of the various spirit beings in which my tribe believes. Tell me what is important to you, to those who remained behind. We can replicate whatever we need to make the ritual feel right to you and your fellow colonists."

Fortier stared at the items, reaching to trace a pattern with a long forefinger. She let him keep the silence until he was ready to break it.

At last, he spoke. "I'm afraid to do this, Sekaya."

"Why?"

"I'm afraid that if we design a ceremony for the dead, then we'll find them dead. I'm afraid that if we design a ceremony that is joyful, Fate will laugh in our faces. It's silly, I know, but there it is."

He turned haunted eyes to her. "I've kept this dream alive for years. More times than I can count, I have imagined transporting down to Loran II and embracing my brother, seeing the buildings—the homes—that we were forced to abandon standing ready and waiting for us. I've asked my people to hang on to that hope. What if it's not there?"

Gently, Sekaya placed a hand on his arm. "Then you grieve. You honor your dead. You decide if you want to stay, and if you do, you start over."

He placed his own hand, strong and warm, over hers and squeezed it gently. "You sound as if you know exactly what that's like."

She looked him full in the eye. "I do, Marius. I do."

Chapter
16

JANEWAY AND TUVOK were not permitted to transport down to the surface of Boreth, but Commander Logt granted permission, albeit grudgingly, for B'Elanna to beam up to say hello to her old friends.

Paris let out something perilously close to a whoop as he and his wife materialized on—

"The *Delta Flyer!*" he exclaimed in delight. "Oh, sweetheart, am I happy to see you!"

"Do I get at least a hello?" came a warm voice.

"Absolutely," Tom said to Admiral Janeway, stepping forward for a handshake and finding himself pulled into a friendly hug. Janeway embraced B'Elanna with equal enthusiasm. Tuvok merely quirked an eyebrow slightly higher than usual.

"Now, B'Elanna, let me see this precious little girl," said Janeway, holding out her arms for Miral. Paris said a small prayer that his daughter would be on her best behavior. You could never tell; sometimes Miral was an angel and sometimes she was . . . well, not. Fortunately, all seemed to be well for the moment, and Miral rewarded Janeway's beaming smile with an intent, focused look. Tom sneaked another look around, pleased beyond his expectations to see the *Flyer* again. His fingers itched to touch the controls, but for the moment, he had to be satisfied with running his hand along the back of a seat.

"My goodness, little one," the admiral said. "You are so much bigger than when I last saw you."

Janeway traced the subtle brow ridges with a finger, smiled as the baby blew a spit bubble, kissed the little hand, and handed the girl back to her mother.

"She's beautiful. How is life on Boreth for the parents of so young a baby?"

"Surprisingly good," said Paris. He told Janeway about the imposing Kularg and his tender care of the children entrusted to him.

"Better than her godfather?" asked Janeway.

Paris's face softened. "Nah," he said, suddenly realizing how much he missed the EMH and his other friends. Six months on Boreth had been a long time. "No one's better with Miral than the Doc. Not even us."

"How's he doing?" asked B'Elanna. "We haven't heard much about any of you here."

Janeway's smile faltered a little. "Less well than we had hoped," she said. "Seven is in her element, of course, as you can imagine, and the Doctor is too, truth be told. But he can't shake his association with Baines and the HoloRevolution."

"Partially," Tuvok interjected, "because he continues to advance his cause."

Paris's blue eyes went cold. "Hey," he said, gently but firmly. "Doc's not a murderer."

"I am not suggesting that he is," replied Tuvok, unflappable as always. "But the Doctor has an agenda that is deeply personal to him, and continues to work toward the desired end."

"He's not in any trouble?" B'Elanna asked. Her brows drew together. "Because if he is—"

"No," Janeway reassured her. "Nothing like that. But Tuvok's right. The Doctor isn't going to let the issue of holographic rights disappear as if it had never been brought up."

"Nor should he," said Paris.

Janeway regarded him, her eyes twinkling. "I see that I have quite a bit of work to do if I'm to polish this gem into a first officer," she said.

Paris felt his face grow hot. "Sorry, Admiral. It's just that—"

"Oh, I agree with you, Tom, and if it were just the four of us—the five of us," she amended, smiling at the baby, "I'd be happy to discuss it with you till the wee hours over coffee. But we're about to get under way for a diplomatic mission, and I think you'd be wise to leave the holographic rights issue, as well as any other particularly controversial subject, at home."

"You're right, of course," Tom said. He hadn't missed the hint she'd dropped and realized that the painful moment of parting with his family had arrived. He and B'Elanna had said a more intimate farewell earlier, and the small confines of the *Flyer* in front of Janeway and Tuvok was hardly the place for a heartfelt good-bye.

So he took their child from her, kissed his little girl sweetly, and bent and kissed his wife on the cheek.

"Make me proud," she said.

"I'll do my best," he said. "Gotta come back to Boreth with honor, right?"

B'Elanna seemed about to say something, hesitated, and then smiled. She caressed his cheek one last time, then stepped back. He was surprised at how his heart ached as they dematerialized.

"Now, Mr. Paris," said Janeway, "You and I need to get down to business."

Sekaya sat on the sun-warmed rock and wept.

Chakotay was gone. He had left with the Starfleet people the day before. Things had not been the same since he and Kolopak had returned from their trip to Earth, despite Kolopak's amazing news about finally meeting the Rubber Tree People. The moment that Sekaya and her mother saw father and son walk up to-

ward the hut, their eyes on the ground and their bodies stiff with tension, the women realized that the trip, intended to bond the two, had only driven them further apart. And when Chakotay announced his decision to leave and attend Starfleet Academy, Sekaya was certain that everyone could hear the sound of her heart breaking.

They had their differences, as all siblings did, but they had always been close. And now he was gone. Wanting to be away from anyone, needing to nurse her grief alone, Sekaya had sought solace in this place. Chakotay had discovered it when they were younger, off carelessly exploring one sunny afternoon, and it was a special place for both of them. Nowhere did she feel closer to her brother than here.

Gradually her sobs ceased, and she wiped her hand across her streaming nose. Even as she did, she smiled at what her parents would say. Such conduct was not becoming of a young woman. Sekaya was almost fifteen, and she should not behave in such a way.

"Sekaya?"

She would know that voice anywhere. Although normally she loved Blue Water Boy's company, he was the last person she wanted to see now. Hastily, Sekaya rose and dove into the little lake so that he would not be able to tell that she had been crying.

When she emerged, she saw him sitting on the rock looking solemnly at her.

"I'm sorry you've been crying," he said. She almost

smiled. It had been silly to think she could slip anything past him. "I will miss Chakotay too. It was always the three of us doing everything together. It will be very different now."

He did seem sad, but also, as always, a bit distant and a little dreamy, as if he wasn't fully present. Sekaya eased herself out of the pool and sat beside him. He seemed not to mind that her wet swimming sarong made a little puddle that expanded to include him. They stared silently into the water, their reflections shimmering into solidity as the surface calmed.

"I don't know what I'll do without him," Sekaya admitted finally. "I feel like half of myself has gone. And it was so sudden, so unexpected. I had no idea."

Blue Water Boy looked at her and smiled. He had grown tall and lanky with the passing of the years, but had lost none of his little-boy sweetness.

"You knew, Sky," he said, using the nickname he'd created as a little boy trying to pronounce her name for the first time. "You just didn't want to know that you knew. He was always trying to get us to talk to the Starfleet officers, imagining scenarios of life on a starship. Chakotay is a contrary. He must always walk the hardest path. That is his destiny. It's a hard fate, but he'll learn much."

He looked back into the water, meeting her reflection's eyes. "And he'll come back."

She snorted. "No, he won't. Even if he wanted to, I doubt Father would let him."

"Your father adores both of you, Sky. They'll mend the rift one day. Chakotay will return. You'll see."

"How do you know?"

He shrugged. "I just do."

And she believed him. Blue Water Boy did "just know" things. It was uncanny, sometimes, and was one reason he was not the most popular among the young men of his tribe. Or the young women; Sekaya never saw him pair off at any of the all-tribe dances. For that matter, neither did she; she, her brother, and Blue Water Boy would always hang around one another rather than socialize with the other young people. When the three of them were together, they knew that they were in the finest of company.

He reached inside the small pack he carried and withdrew his flute. He was hardly ever without the instrument. He held it in his hands for a moment, stroking the dark, polished wood reverently.

"When I learned Chakotay was leaving," he said quietly, still staring raptly at the flute, "I wept for him too. But I wept with music, not tears. Do you want to hear it, Sekaya, during your nuanka?"

Her throat closed up so that words could not creep past the lump, so she merely nodded. Blue Water Boy made a song for everything—for the dawn in the morning, the hatching of eggs, a good hunt, a starlit night. The songs were always exquisite, and Sekaya both dreaded and feared the power of the music that would issue from the carved wooden instrument.

CHRISTIE GOLDEN

A breeze ruffled his dark hair as he brought the flute to his lips and began to play. Sekaya listened, the tears returning. Blue Water Boy had not been speaking metaphorically when he said that he wept with his music. The clear, haunting sound wrapped around Sekaya like a woven blanket, tears transformed into musical notes, and, heedless of how immature she would appear to her childhood friend, she wept while he played. How long they both sat and grieved, each in his or her own way, she didn't know, but at last, she felt as though all her tears had been cried.

Blue Water Boy put away his flute and resumed staring quietly into the lake's surface. Sekaya's heart still ached for the loss of her brother's presence, but now, somehow, she found that it beat a little faster. She continued to regard Blue Water Boy's face in the water; it was always pleasant to look upon, but now it was handsome, a young man's face. He, too, looked at her, and her breathing suddenly quickened. Abruptly, she was shy around this young man. And Sekaya was never shy.

She dragged her gaze away from the water and looked directly into Blue Water Boy's eyes. She saw in them gentleness, wonder, and the same odd shyness she was feeling.

"Sky," he said softly, his voice trembling slightly.

She closed her eyes and leaned forward, giving the honor of her first kiss to this sweet boy she had loved all her life, who pressed his lips to hers with at first a kind of hesitant awe, then with increasing passion, not dreamy and distant from her, not anymore. . . .

"Chakotay to Sekaya."

Sekaya bolted awake, heart hammering. Where was she? She took in the room and realized that she had fallen asleep. Collecting herself, she tapped her combadge and replied, "Sekaya here. What is it, Chakotay?"

"We're about to enter orbit around Loran II. Thought you'd want to be on the bridge when we drop out of warp."

"I do indeed. I'm on my way." She ran a quick brush through her hair, slipped on her shoes, deliberately banished thoughts of Blue Water Boy and their first kiss, and headed for the turbolift.

Chapter

17

BY THE TIME Sekaya reached the bridge, Fortier and Astall were already there. Fortier greeted Sekaya with a brief smile, then returned his gaze to the viewscreen. He folded his arms tightly against his body. Astall's ears flapped gently, betraying her agitation.

Chakotay nodded to his sister, then gave the command. "Helm, drop out of warp and establish orbit around Loran II."

"Aye, Captain." Smoothly, Tare complied.

"Campbell, put it on-screen."

Campbell touched her controls, and Loran II appeared on the huge screen. It was a beautiful planet; its brown and green landmasses and lush oceans reminded

Chakotay of Earth, the place that even now he thought of as home.

"There's a lot of debris floating around here still, all of it old," said Kim.

"Captain," said Campbell, "there seems to be an extremely active storm system centered over a small part of the northern hemisphere."

Chakotay frowned. "Let's see it."

For a moment, everyone stared at the huge storm system slowly turning. It looked like a hurricane or a cyclone.

"But . . . that's exactly where our colony is!" exclaimed Fortier.

"Lieutenant, attempt to hail the colony."

"No response, sir," Campbell said. "Readings are inconclusive but . . ." She hesitated, then said, "But there seem to be no humanoid life readings anywhere on the planet." She touched the controls. "I'm picking up some kind of surge. . . . It could be a natural phenomenon, but it has a pretty high EM reading." She grimaced slightly. "And I should tell you we've been having trouble with the ops system before—a ghost or two in the works."

Chakotay gazed at the strange storm, frowning. There was something oddly familiar about this, but he couldn't put his finger on it.

"Mr. Fortier, what sort of research did your colony perform?"

Fortier had swallowed hard at Campbell's announce-

CHRISTIE GOLDEN

ment, but spoke calmly. "The usual—biological, geological, meteorological."

"Did you have any sort of weather-control technology?" Chakotay asked. It wasn't unheard of; it was how Risa managed to maintain its tourist base.

Fortier shook his dark head. "No. We studied the weather, of course, just like we studied everything else on the planet. But we made no attempts to control it."

"Were storms like this common?"

Fortier turned to him. "Captain," he said quietly, "I've never seen anything like this before in my life."

"Lieutenant, is this a natural or a created storm?" asked Chakotay.

"I'm not detecting anything that leads me to believe it's artificial," Campbell replied. "But if I may speak freely, sir, the fact that it happens to be located directly above the only area with technology seems too coincidental for this to be natural."

"Captain," said Kim, "if the Cardassians did occupy the planet at any point, this might be something they established."

"That would make sense," Campbell said, nodding. "This signal could very well be a by-product of weather control technology in operation."

"Yes," said Sekaya in an odd voice, staring at the image. Her arms, like Fortier's, were folded tightly across her chest. "Yes, the Cardassians did things like that."

Chakotay gave her a sharp look, but she continued to

212

gaze at the screen. He rubbed his chin, considering his words carefully.

"Mr. Fortier, depending on what we find down there, it might be a good idea for you to consider reestablishing the colony elsewhere."

Fortier whirled on Chakotay. "Absolutely not! That is our home, Captain. We had our children there." His throat worked. "It now seems likely that we will bury our dead there. We must find out what happened. And when we do, we'll reclaim this place and make it thrive again. None of us has any desire to start all over again somewhere else, no matter . . . no matter what we might find down there."

Chakotay searched his eyes for a moment. He hoped that Fortier's desire would be possible to fulfill. But Chakotay's would be the final decision. He was under orders to keep the colonists safe, above everything else. If that meant forcing them to relocate elsewhere on Loran II, or even insisting they abandon the planet altogether, he knew he'd do it.

"Before we make any final decisions," Chakotay said, "I've got to make sure it's safe. Mr. Ellis, you're to lead the away team."

Ellis did a double take. Chakotay smothered a smile. He'd never seen his first officer look more surprised.

"Begging your pardon, Captain, but I assumed you'd be the one to lead an away team," he said.

"I'm not quite the rebel that you and many in Starfleet think, Mr. Ellis," he said, still smiling but also very serious. "It's my first mission and I'm going by the book. I'm sure you of all people can appreciate that."

Ellis continued to look nonplussed. The smile faded from Chakotay's face. "In case you're not sure, Mr. Ellis, that's an order."

Ellis nodded quickly. "Of course, sir. I was just— Sorry, sir. Do you have any, uh, recommendations as to whom you want on the team?"

"It'll be your team and your mission, Commander. Assemble whomever you think would be best."

Astall was fully aware that, like every member of her species, she was poor at hiding her emotions. So she concentrated intently on keeping her "Federation ears" on and staring straight ahead when she got into the turbolift with Sekaya, Ellis, and Fortier. Fortunately, they were talking intently among themselves, and she got off first. She scurried down the hall to sickbay and burst in on Kaz.

"Good, you're alone."

His lips twitched in amusement. "Well, hello, Astall. What can I—"

She waved her hands for silence. "Kaz, listen to me. I just came from the bridge. We've just had our first look at Loran II. While it doesn't appear that there were any battles fought there, we weren't able to detect any signs of human life."

Kaz's smile faded. "Damn," he said, sighing. "That's a blow."

Astall wanted to let her eyes fill with sympathetic tears on behalf of the colonists, but refused to surrender to her emotions.

"But there was also a strange storm system that might well be artificial. Lieutenant Campbell said that it's entirely possible that something was interfering with our sensors. It's likely that Ellis will want you on the away team, in case they encounter any wounded," she finished.

"Likely? Try certain. Thanks for the heads up, I'll assemble a kit."

"Jarem, you have to tell Chakotay. Tell him about what we did."

He had been moving quickly, but now he froze. He turned to look at her.

"What we did," he said coldly, "won't interfere with the performance of my duty as a doctor. I told you that."

"But Chakotay needs to know about it. There are others who can—"

His handsome, expressive face shut down. "No. I'm not going to tell him."

"It's one thing for you to operate on *Voyager,*" she continued, wringing her hands and bouncing slightly in her agitation. "I have no doubts whatsoever about your ability to function here."

"Why, thank you, your confidence is overwhelming."

Astall cringed. She hated sarcasm. To the sensitive Huanni, it often felt like a physical blow.

"But you'll be going down in the middle of a storm," she continued gamely. "To a colony. To a place where

215

there could be Cardassian technology. There could be all kinds of triggers that could distress Gradak. I think you'll be all right, frankly, and you seem to think so too. But we must let Chakotay know. He needs to make an informed decision. Surely you understand the need for that. It's the right thing to do."

Kaz turned away abruptly, but not before she saw his jaw tighten. She wondered what humanoids would think if they knew how easily Huanni could read them. Their body language and facial expressions, even that of the most reserved of them, told the story more eloquently than their words did. Even Vulcans weren't immune to Huanni scrutiny. As highly emotional creatures themselves, Huanni were attuned to any signals from others.

Right now, she could easily see that Jarem Kaz was torn. He was wise enough to understand Gradak's need to be healed, but embarrassed that he couldn't control feelings that were welling up inside him, yet were not his own. He was fond of Chakotay and Janeway and wanted so much to prove his worth to them. He had a stubborn pride that didn't want to admit that right now, he might not be able to do what he could be called on to do, and he had the will to see it through.

Finally, he turned to her. "All right. But I want you there. I want him to hear it from us both."

Astall let out a gusty sigh of relief and had to almost physically stop herself from hugging him.

"Let's go."

*   *   *

216

Chakotay was surprised to hear from both his counselor and his doctor, but agreed to meet them in his ready room.

"So, what's this all about?" he asked as the door hissed closed behind them. He indicated the sofa and they sat, perched uneasily on the edge. They exchanged glances.

Finally, Kaz spoke. "Chakotay— Damn, this is hard to put into words." Chakotay waited patiently. Kaz hesitated, searching for an opening, and finally said, "You know about Gradak."

"Your symbiont's previous host? The Maquis? Of course. What about him?"

"Remember we talked a little when you came in for your physical?"

Comprehension dawned. So that was why his physician and his counselor wanted to see him in private. . . .

"Ah," Chakotay said. "He's doing more than stirring a bit then, is he?"

"It was my suggestion," Astall blurted out. "I thought it might help if we brought Gradak's memories to the forefront and let him tell us what happened to him. It's almost as if Jarem was suffering from post-traumatic stress disorder that wasn't his own."

Kaz clasped and unclasped his hands. Chakotay wanted to set his friend's mind at ease, so he said, "Isn't there some sort of ritual that the Trill perform to isolate the personalities of the former hosts?"

"The *zhian'tara*," Jarem replied. "It's a pretty complicated ritual and takes some time to prepare for. It's not something we can do here and now, but Astall did bring Gradak to the forefront of my thoughts."

"The problem is," said Astall, "there ought to have been plenty of time for Jarem to finish the guided meditation, hear Gradak out, and then rest and recover. Gradak would have been satisfied, and Jarem would no longer be distracted."

"But we got to Loran II too fast for that," said Chakotay, nodding.

"Yes," said Kaz. "And while I feel completely capable, Astall thought that you should know what's going on with me. And upon reflection, I think she was right to insist. It's your call, sir."

Chakotay looked from one to the other, considering. He was no stranger to spirit walks, which were very similar to what Kaz had undergone with Astall. But this was different; the spirits didn't accompany you back to the "real" world the way Gradak obviously had.

"So you feel competent to perform your duties, Kaz?"

"I do, sir."

"Even with a dead Maquis knocking around in your skull?"

Kaz had to smile a little at that. "Even so, sir."

Chakotay nodded. "Astall, what's your professional opinion?"

"Right now, I think the doctor is fully capable, sir. I'll keep an eye on him, and the moment I think he's not, I'll relieve him of duty."

"I'd relieve myself first, sir," Kaz said, quickly and earnestly.

"Okay," said Chakotay. "Here are my thoughts. I trust you both. Astall, if you agree with Jarem that he is fit to continue with his duty, then I have no problem with him doing so. But I do want you to keep an eye on him."

Kaz relaxed slightly. Astall flopped back onto the sofa with a loud "Whew!" Chakotay grinned.

"I only thought that being on the away team might distress the doctor somewhat. Not that I didn't think he could handle it," she added swiftly.

"Well, that won't be an issue," said Chakotay. "The away team has already left."

"What?" Kaz's voice was loud and sharp. "You're not leading it? And I'm not going?"

"Me either?" piped up Astall.

"I thought that I'd give it to Pri—to Ellis. And he didn't seem to think he'd need either of you."

Kaz stared at him. "Chakotay, with this storm messing up our sensors, you can't be certain they're accurate. How do you know there won't be wounded down there?"

"It was Ellis's call. Not the call I'd make, but frankly, we lost contact with the colonists several months ago. I don't think anything we discover will be an emergency situation." He looked at them intently. "Do you?"

Sighing, Kaz shook his head. "Unfortunately, no."

Softly, Astall added, "Nor does Fortier. He wants to believe they're still alive, of course, but . . ." She blinked quickly.

"Ellis took Kim, Patel, and a security team with him. We can't transport because of the electrical storm, so he took a shuttle. He will assess the situation and report back. If it turns out there is an emergency, we can get another shuttle down there quickly enough."

Kaz stood. "Very well, sir," he said, adding quietly, "I hope you're right."

They stepped out of the ready room onto the bridge. Campbell, who had been sitting in the captain's chair in Chakotay's absence, yielded it gracefully and returned to her station.

"Thank you, Captain," said Kaz.

"Any time," Chakotay told him and Astall as they headed for the turbolift.

He turned to Campbell. "Any word yet from Commander Ellis, Lieutenant?"

"Negative, sir."

Chakotay nodded, and stared at the screen thoughtfully. The storm still swirled.

"Campbell," he asked slowly, "what do you make of this?"

She shook her head. "Truthfully? I don't know, sir. It's unusual, but we've still seen nothing to indicate it's artificial. Perhaps Commander Ellis will be able to get us more data."

"Has it changed at all?"

"Negative, Captain."

"That's unusual for a storm, isn't it?"

Campbell regarded him with intent blue eyes. "Highly," she replied.

"Highly unusual," he repeated, more to himself than to her. He'd seen something like this before, in the Delta Quadrant. A storm that seemed peculiarly localized and inconvenient. Why couldn't he remember which mission?

Because you've been on a few thousand, he thought, both amused and annoyed.

"Campbell, search the databanks and see if you run across anything similar. I've got a strange sense of déjà vu about this."

To his surprise, she said, "I've got that same feeling, sir. I think we've seen this before. I'll see what I can come up with."

"Commander Ellis to *Voyager.*"

"Go ahead."

"We're about to enter the storm system, sir. Lieutenant Patel wanted us to get some concrete readings before we enter the system. She seems to think it likely that we might lose contact."

"Lieutenant Patel," asked Chakotay, "what are your thoughts about this storm?"

Devi Patel's voice replied, "Captain, it's my opinion that—"

There was a sharp burst of static, then silence.

Patel had been right—they had lost contact with the shuttle.

Chapter
18

"CAPTAIN, it's my opinion that—"

Kim never did learn Patel's opinion. At that moment there was a terrible noise and the shuttle bucked like a wild horse. The small Patel was thrown from her seat. Kim, Ellis, and security officers Brendan Niemann and Kathryn Kaylar barely managed to hang on to theirs.

Ellis, grim-faced, struggled with the controls in an effort to keep the shuttle stable. Not for the first time on this mission, Kim wished they still had the good old *Delta Flyer* at their command. The sleek little ship designed by three friends was, as far as he knew, still at McKinley Station being picked apart. He wondered it if would be the same when they got it back.

Another round of turbulence shook the little vessel.

As he picked himself up off the floor, Kim wondered if *he'd* be the same.

"Altitude five thousand meters," he said, easing quickly back into his seat.

"Decreasing speed to seven hundred twenty kph," said Ellis. He didn't sound at all perturbed. "Entering terminal approach phase."

"Visibility still zero," said Kim, glowering at the viewscreen, which revealed nothing but swirling gray. "Switching to enhanced terrain scanning."

Ellis nodded. "Touchdown site scanned," he confirmed. "Continuing descent."

Through the haze of clouds, Kim could finally start to make out the ground approaching.

Fast.

"Hang on!" Ellis cried.

They landed roughly, but the shuttle appeared to be still intact. The emergency lighting went on as the crew picked themselves up. Kim flexed his hand and grimaced; he had probably sprained his wrist. Other than that, he seemed to be intact. He glanced around, trying to assess any injuries. Kaylar was rubbing a knee and wincing, but the injury didn't seem to be anything more serious than a bump. Patel had sustained a bruised shoulder and had a small cut on her forehead.

"You're bleeding," said Kim.

Patel touched the cut. "It's nothing," she said.

"That's a lot of blood, and you might have sustained a head injury," Kim said. He reached for the medkit.

"No, really, it's nothing. Head wounds bleed a lot," said Patel, still protesting, but she permitted Harry to quickly tend the wound.

"Everyone else all right?" Ellis asked. Kim thought he sounded a bit impatient.

"I think so," said Kim. "You okay, Kaylar? Niemann?"

The two security officers nodded. Just to be sure, Kim scanned them quickly too. He took care of his sprained wrist in a few seconds, then ran a quick check on himself to see if he'd unwittingly suffered anything more severe. He started to scan Ellis. Scowling in annoyance, the first officer slapped away the little instrument.

"For goodness' sake, Lieutenant, I'm fine!" he growled. "Lieutenant Patel, report."

The diminutive science officer had returned to her seat and was scanning the area outside.

"Curious," she said, her eyes narrowing. "The storm seems to have stopped. For the moment." She touched a few more controls. "It's still covering almost exactly the same square kilometers as before, but there's a lot of fluctuation within that area."

She looked up at Ellis. "We may want to scan hay while the sun shines."

Kim, Niemann, and Kaylar all groaned goodnaturedly at the word play, but the little joke seemed to only irritate Ellis further. Kaz had told Harry—confidentially, of course—that in certain circles Ellis had acquired the nickname Priggy. Kim was starting to under-stand why.

"Phasers on stun," ordered Ellis. Kim and the two security guards exchanged slightly guilty glances; they'd both already pulled out their phasers without waiting for their commanding officer to issue the order.

The shuttle door hissed open. Humidity assaulted them. It was still overcast and the vegetation steamed and dripped, but Patel had been right. The storm had indeed moved on—for the moment.

"Regulation disembarkation," said Ellis crisply. Kim tried not to roll his eyes. He hadn't heard that order since his Academy days. Ellis led the way, followed by Kim, Niemann, Kaylar, and Patel. Kim's boots sank slightly in the waterlogged soil. The air smelled fresh and crisp. All in all, it was very pleasant.

Patel scrutinized her tricorder. "Any humanoid life signs?" asked Ellis.

Patel examined the readings, shook her head, and sighed. "Still negative, sir. I think we were clinging to false hope, thinking that somehow the storm was inter-fering with our sensors."

Kim felt his spirits sink. Damn it. He hadn't realized until now how much he hoped they'd find the colonists alive and well, even though he knew such an outcome was doubtful.

Ellis sighed. "That's too bad." He tapped his com-badge. "Ellis to *Voyager.*"

"Good to hear from you, Commander. I take it you were able to land safely?"

Kim continued to look about with a watchful eye. According to the colonists, this planet was not without its share of large predators, though they weren't common and the colonists said no one had ever been attacked. Kaylar and Niemann, too, stayed alert, their phasers out. Patel continued to take scans. Her own phaser was on her hip; clearly she was one of those scientific types who could easily become engrossed in what she was doing.

"Aye, Captain," Ellis continued. "But I regret to inform you that we have some bad news for Mr. Fortier and the rest of the colonists. I'm sorry to say that it still doesn't look as if there are any survivors. The storm or whatever Campbell was picking up wasn't interfering with our sensors after all. The storm, by the way, appears to have moved off for the time being."

Silence. Then, "I can't say I expected anything else, but it's definitely sad news. I'll inform Fortier."

"Captain," said Patel, "the storm appears to be quite erratic. It's not raining on us at the moment, but that could change at any moment. We'll take what readings we can when we can."

"Understood. Keep me posted. Chakotay out."

Ellis pursed his lips and thought. "The settlement is a half kilometer or so to the east, if I'm not mistaken." He shot Patel a look.

"Correct, sir."

"I don't see the point in taking the shuttle for such a short distance. The hike will do us all good, and if there's a sudden squall, we can take shelter in the settlement. I want you to fan out in standard exploration pattern Beta Four Three Four. You all have tricorders; keep track of your direction and of one another. We will reconvene at fifteen hundred hours at the center of the colony. I believe there's a town square that will suit our purposes. You will be searching for any and all of the following threats that might prevent the colonists from resettling."

To Kim's disbelief, Ellis actually began to tick them off on his fingers. "Any hostile life-forms. Any indications that the area has been booby-trapped by the Cardassians or the Dominion or any other adversarial species. Any buildings that are unsafe. Any radiation or climatic changes. And anything else that you think might be worth reporting. Understood?"

"Aye, sir," said Kim, Patel, Kaylar, and Niemann in chorus. Kim thought they sounded like the good crew of the H.M.S. *Pinafore*.

"Very good. I'll see you all at fifteen hundred hours, then." Ellis strode off boldly and was soon swallowed up by the forest.

Kim sighed and looked at the other three. "I'm not overly fond of standard exploration pattern Beta Four Three Four," he told his team. "I don't like to separate a group in an unknown situation. But we have our orders, and so far things don't appear too dangerous. So let's do it. See you in a couple of hours. Keep on your toes."

The lights were bright, almost blinding, blocking the view of hundreds of people sitting in the audience. Libby was always grateful for that. It was best when she could just sink into the music and not have to think about "performing." And that state was most easily accomplished when she couldn't see her audience.

Even so, she often closed her eyes and surrendered to the exquisite sounds of the *lal-shak* as she coaxed forth its voice with her long, strong fingers. Somewhere between a harp, a cello, and a lute, the stringed instrument produced a sound unlike anything she had ever heard. This was why she had fallen in love with Ktarian music as a young woman; this was what held her even now and made her forget her other, less spiritual duties.

Sweat beaded her brow, trickled down her sides, dewed her throat. She loved it. Her breathing was deep and even, but her heart raced as it always did.

Her fingers flew. The *lal-shak* sang. Libby fell even more firmly under its spell.

The music spun faster from her hands, faster still in this piece that was a challenge even for native players to perform. There were no coughing or rustling sounds from the audience to disenchant the entranced woman, and she didn't miss a note or a beat. The piece built to its crescendo, exploded, and then there was silence.

She opened her eyes at the first sound of the applause. It pattered like rain on her ears, punctuated with whoops and whistles. Shaking with the exertion, Libby rose and bowed to the audience. She was smiling so hard it hurt, but she couldn't stop grinning. This was the second reason she continued to perform—this profound, heartfelt connection with her audiences. She moved them with her playing, and in return, they expressed their joy and gratitude. It was a satisfying, nourishing cycle.

She bowed again and again. An assistant came onstage to respectfully take her instrument so she would have her hands free to wave and blow kisses to the audience that didn't appear to want to stop clapping anytime soon. Then the flowers appeared on the stage: roses, orchids, bushels of the exquisite *sayayan* that she once told an interviewer were her favorite. They would all be gathered up and given to the hardworking members of her touring group, as her tiny cabin could hold only so many flowers.

Finally, the lights dimmed and she left the stage. She gulped the glass of water that her assistant, Stephanie, held out to her and permitted herself to be ushered back to her changing room.

"You were amazing tonight!" Stephanie said. "You were on fire, Libby. Fantastic."

She helped the other woman out of her long blue gown.

"Thanks, Steph," Libby said. "I feel absolutely wrung out."

"You give everything to your performance," Stephanie said. "Don't you save anything for yourself?"

"Not usually," Libby admitted. She stepped into the sonic shower and let it remove all traces of dirt and sweat. She emerged a few moments later clean, but not really revived. She was a water baby and preferred showers and baths, where one actually got wet.

Libby slipped into the fresh, more casual outfit Stephanie held up for her and began to reapply her makeup.

"What's the schedule tonight?" Libby asked.

"Party afterwards at the director's place," Stephanie said, brushing Libby's long, curly hair.

"Who's attending?" Libby tried to keep her voice casual, but she always worried that she would give herself away.

"Let me see. . . ." Stephanie paused in her brushing and quickly examined a padd. "Not a lot of military brass at this one."

Inwardly, Libby frowned. She needed every social engagement to forward her investigation, but she couldn't risk asking too many people to attend such small gatherings.

"Admiral Montgomery—he sent the two dozen

white roses, hard to get here—Admiral Jorgensen, and Captains Skhaa and Nunez."

Libby perked up at the mention of the middle two names. These were two on her "list."

"Well, that's not too big a crowd to work, even as tired as I am," she told Stephanie.

As she finished applying her cosmetics and permitted Stephanie to play with her thick, wild locks and give them some semblance of order, Libby's mind worked furiously. She was doing her utmost to remember names and dates and data. If she could determine where Jorgensen and Shkaa were on particular dates, she could exonerate them or else confirm her suspicion that they were somehow involved.

But she had to ask herself now as she had every day for the last several days—involved in what?

Sekaya was surprised at how devastated she was when Chakotay gave her the news. They had all been expecting this, even if they didn't want to say so, but his quiet words made her eyes fill with tears.

"Those poor people," she said softly, a shaky hand covering her mouth. He rose and went to her, folding his strong arms around her. She closed her eyes and nestled into him. She had missed him so.

"This seems to have really upset you," he said, pulling away from her slightly and looking into her eyes. "Sekky, I know we've got a lot on our plate right now, but you've got to tell me what happened on Dorvan V."

"I will," she promised him. An image of Blue Water Boy rose in her memory and she almost started crying again. "But that's history, and Loran II's colonists are suffering now. I need to talk to them."

"They're all in the cargo bay," he said. "Astall is with them. They're expecting you." He kissed the top of her head. "Go to them. I hope you have some comfort to give them."

"I do too," Sekaya said.

She had imagined that by this time in their journey, she would be seeing Fortier and the other colonists finally in the place that they had called home, wandering the hills and fields, gathering in the small town they had built themselves. Instead, they were in the impersonal cargo bay of a starship, clustered together as if huddling against a raging storm outside.

Fortier was kneeling and talking to an older woman when Sekaya entered. Sekaya could tell the woman had been crying, but had now wiped her face and was nodding at something Fortier said. At the sound of the door opening, Fortier glanced up. His dark gaze locked with Sekaya's, and she saw by his reddened eyes that he, too, had shed tears for the fallen. He'd lost a brother, after all. His show of love and compassion moved her.

She strode quickly to him and they embraced. Sekaya wasn't sure how this bond had formed. She barely knew Marius Fortier, but unknown to him, they had a kinship of shared suffering.

There was nothing in the embrace but affection, compassion, and concern. Sekaya thought this a good thing. She did not want the leader of the colonists to develop a romantic attachment to her. They stepped back and looked up at one another.

"I just heard the news from my brother," she said. "Marius, I grieve with you."

"Thank you, Sekaya. It's not as if we weren't expecting it, but . . . Well." He sighed and straightened himself. "I see you've brought something," he said, indicating the bulging pack she had slung over her shoulder.

"Yes," she replied. "Some of the things we talked about for the ritual."

"Ah, yes. The ritual. Well, I think we know which one we're going to be performing."

"Performing *first*," Sekaya corrected.

"Pardon?"

She smiled a little, sadly. "We know that first it is time to grieve," she said. "To mourn your dead and salute them. But then, we'll need to perform the other ritual we created. The one to say hello again to this place that you love. Am I not right?"

He seemed startled that she understood him so well. "Are we so easy to read?"

"Yes and no," she said. "Easy for one who understands you, perhaps."

He nodded. "Yes, Sekaya. Yes, you are right. What

was it you said? We will grieve, and decide if we want to stay, and start over."

He extended a hand. Confused but willing to go along with him, Sekaya took it. He led her into the cargo bay. Seeing the two of them approach, the colonists got to their feet and looked at her curiously. Still holding her hand, Fortier said, "Some of you have not yet had the honor and pleasure of meeting Sekaya. I have been talking with her about ceremonies. Traditions. Things that matter to our people. She has some ideas."

Sekaya took a moment before she spoke. She looked around the crowd, at the sad yet determined faces. She felt a rush of warmth, of kinship with these strangers.

"We humans need ritual," she said. "We need celebrations, and ways to mark important passages. We need," she said quietly, "to be able to say good-bye."

Damn it, where had they encountered a storm like this before?

Chakotay was alone in his ready room, hoping the solitude would help him focus. He drummed his fingers on his thigh. He couldn't remember. But it had been the precursor to something very important. And it was similar, but not exact. . . . There was something about trying to transport to a specific site and storms appearing precisely at that site. . . .

He was so lost in his thoughts that he started when he heard Ellis's voice.

"Ellis to Captain Chakotay."

Chakotay sat upright. There was a strained sound to the commander's voice.

"Go ahead, Ellis."

"I, uh . . . sir, there's something very odd here that I think you ought to see. I'm taking a scan of it and I'm going to try to transmit it to you. I hope there won't be too much interference. I'm not overly familiar with the customs of our passengers, but this somehow doesn't look like something the colonists would do, and it's clearly not Cardassian. But it's recent."

"You are definitely whetting my curiosity, Commander. Go ahead and transmit." He touched a button. The image appeared on the small viewscreen.

Chakotay inhaled swiftly, his eyes widening in shock.

He knew that image. Knew it from when he was fifteen years old, walking with his father on Earth in the Central American rain forest. Recognized it when he saw it drawn on the dust of a moon, many years and several thousand light-years away from that first encounter.

A blessing to the land.

A *chamozi*.

Chapter
19

LIBBY WEBBER STEPPED into her director's home to the sound of applause. She smiled and waved slightly at the assembled crowd and accepted yet another bouquet with graciousness.

A large man stepped up to her and kissed her on the cheek. "Admiral Montgomery! How good to see you!" she said.

"Ken, Libby, Ken. It's only 'admiral' when the pips are there to insist upon it." Indeed, he was out of uniform and looked quite dashing in his tuxedo, his weathered face split in a grin.

As far as he knew, they had met only a few months ago at one of her concerts. Kim had introduced them and they hit it off immediately. Libby, though, had once thought that Admiral Montgomery was at worst a traitor to the Federation, at best a cranky old geezer whose ultimate goal in life was to stand in the way of the *Voyager* crew. He had proven his worth in the end, and thus won Libby's affections. Now she regarded him fondly as a sort of burly uncle whose gruff manner hid a great heart.

"Very well, Ken," she acquiesced. "I understand it was you who sent me the white roses. Thank you so much, they're beautiful."

"You're very welcome, my dear. Come, let me introduce you around." Libby threw a wry glance at her director, Philippe Batiste, who shrugged in a very Gallic way. He'd just been trumped by Montgomery—as had so many others—but as his gesture said, what could one do?

They made the rounds, Montgomery introducing Libby to a truly impressive variety of important personages. Libby had done her research and was able to speak intelligently with each of them. She loved this part of her job; she was naturally a people person and truly enjoyed meeting and talking with others. They always sensed her sincerity, and most of them opened up quickly. More than once Libby had been told that she would have made an excellent diplomat. She had always smiled and expressed thanks for the compliment, claiming devotion to her music.

"And this is Admiral Leah Jorgensen," Montgomery was saying. Libby smiled warmly at the wiry, attractive woman who extended both a hand and a grin. She wore her straight gray-streaked hair short and didn't use a great deal of cosmetics. Her nails were filed short, and while well-manicured, were not polished. This, Libby thought, was what tomboys looked like when they grew up. Their eyes met, and she liked Leah at once. Her instincts were usually pretty good; Libby hoped that she wasn't a mole.

But there was something familiar . . . "Have we met?" Libby asked.

"We've never been formally introduced, but I'm quite a fan of your music," Jorgensen said. "I've attended as many of your concerts as my schedule permits. You may have seen me in the crowd." Her eyes danced. "I'm a little old to be begging for autographs, so I never approached you."

Libby laughed. She knew she'd seen this woman before. Thinking quickly, she said, "I'm sure your schedule doesn't allow for much concert-going, Admiral. For instance, I'm sure you were expected to be at the Kavlian Peace Conference."

She'd seen Jorgensen's name as an attendee on one of the many documents she'd perused. The admiral sighed. "Yes, I was there. Have you ever met a Kavlian, Miss Webber?"

"Libby, please. Can't say I've had the pleasure."

Jorgensen wrinkled her pert nose. "Can't say it *is* a pleasure. Difficult people to negotiate with. They could have a Royal Protocol document all to themselves."

Montgomery grimaced as well. "I was at that conference. By the end of it, I was about ready to trade being an admiral for being an ensign, if it meant getting to leave a day early."

Libby was enjoying the conversation, but she had now cleared Jorgensen from her list. The woman was where Libby's research had placed her, and Montgomery had just corroborated her story. Now she was anxious to see the other suspect, one Captain Skhaa.

She coughed a little and said, "A little frog in my throat. I think I need something to drink. A pleasure to meet you, Admiral. Excuse me for just a moment—"

Libby scurried off in the direction of a waiter carrying a tray of beverages and snagged a mineral water. No alcohol when she was working. She sipped the beverage and looked around quickly. Skhaa wouldn't be hard to find, he was probably the only avian here—

And there he was, talking with two Vulcans. She recognized one of them as an ambassador she knew, which gave her an opening.

"Ambassador Sular," she said politely; one didn't gush to a Vulcan. "I didn't know you were here tonight."

The tall, elderly Vulcan turned toward her, his elegant robes rustling with the movement. He inclined his head. "Miss Webber. The reason for our presence," he said. "May I introduce my assistant, Korvik, and my friend, Captain Skhaa."

The avian humanoid turned toward her. His species was covered in soft, small, downy feathers, much the way that humans were covered with hair that was much finer than that of the apes from which they had evolved. Otherwise, he looked completely human.

"I was invited to play at the reception for the ambassadors when your world was accepted into the Federation," she said. "Unfortunately, I had a commitment elsewhere. I'm so sorry I couldn't attend."

Skhaa's lips parted in a smile. "The Vulcans very kindly took care of the musical performance, Miss Webber. I enjoy the Vulcan lyre, but I'm sure your presence would have been much . . . livelier."

Libby laughed at the little joke, bowing her head slightly to Sular to let him know she respected him and his people even as she indulged in a little teasing. "I love the Vulcan lyre," she said, "but I do think it sounds the sweetest when Vulcans play it. Were you at that concert, Captain?"

"Indeed I was." He launched into a recitation of the musical numbers performed, but Libby listened with only half an ear.

That night was one of the dates on which someone had accessed *Voyager*'s logs.

That someone was allegedly Captain Skhaa.

But how could he have done so from a concert hall?

"Come in," Chakotay said when when Sekaya stepped into his ready room.

"What's this about?" she asked, walking over to where he sat. Wordlessly, Chakotay showed her the screen. When she saw the familiar symbol of their people, she uttered a small cry.

"Great Spirit, how can this be?" she whispered, gripping her brother's shoulder.

Ellis had found the *chamozi* inscribed on a large, flat stone only a few yards from the deserted buildings that made up the central part of the colony. The localized rainstorms had not passed over the area to wash away the chalk blessing.

It was all starting to add up. Now Chakotay remembered where *Voyager* had previously encountered a similar, specific "storm system." It had been on the planet where Chakotay had met with the Sky Spirits, the aliens who had given his people a genetic "inheritance" forty-five thousand years ago. In that situation, the storms had cropped up every time and in every place where *Voyager* had tried to transport or to land a shuttle. Here, the storm had centered directly over the colony. It was a small difference, but it had been enough to throw Chakotay off track.

"I don't understand it, sir," came Ellis's voice. "This symbol was drawn in chalk. It couldn't have been here for more than a few days. Yet there are no signs of humanoids present on the planet, nor do we have any reason to think there are any nonhumanoid species sufficiently developed to have produced this."

"You won't detect anything if the Sky Spirits are down there," said Chakotay to his first officer. "They won't want you to."

There was a pause. "I beg your pardon, Captain?"

Chakotay and Sekaya exchanged smiles. "It's a long story, Ellis. Sekaya and I are going to take a shuttle down to look at this for ourselves."

Sekaya beamed happily.

"Your sister? With all due respect, Captain, I'm not sure that's a good idea. We have not completed the security sweep of the area yet, and I wouldn't want a civilian exposed to—".

"I'm pulling rank on this one, Ellis."

Again there came a silence, this one stiff and uncomfortable. At last, Ellis resumed.

"Of course, sir. Will you be authorizing the transport of the colonists as well, then?"

"Negative. I've got a lot of questions that need answering before I'm ready for that. We're heading for the shuttlebay now. Send the coordinates to Campbell and we'll meet you there soon." To his sister, he said, "You know what our father would do right now, don't you?"

When Chakotay had returned to Dorvan V to visit his family, he had informed Sekaya about his meeting with the Sky Spirits. She had been thrilled by the story of the encounter, and they had both expressed regret that their father had not been alive to hear of it. Now she smiled back at him, her eyes bright with excitement.

"He'd put on his battered old expedition hat and say, 'Let's go.' "

*   *   *

As they stood in the turbolift, Sekaya said, "I should tell Marius where I'm going."

"It's Marius now, is it?" her brother grinned at her.

She blushed a little, then looked down. "We . . . have a lot in common. It seemed silly to keep using titles—we're both civilians, after all."

"I'm just teasing, Sekky. Let me do it." He tapped his combadge. "Chakotay to Fortier."

"Fortier here. What is it, Captain?"

"We've had a report of discoveries on Loran II of archeological interest," said Chakotay. "Sekaya and I are going to investigate them. My first officer and his team are continuing to check out the planet to see if it's safe for rehabitation by your people. We'll let you know as soon as we hear from him."

"Please do, Captain. Sekaya has given us much food for thought, but we are anxious to take our *nuanka* directly to our home. We cannot have closure until we are there. I trust you understand."

Chakotay raised an eyebrow at Fortier's usage of a word that had originated with Chakotay's tribe.

"I do indeed, Mr. Fortier. You and your people are the reason for this mission. I won't forget you, but do understand that your safety is our top priority."

"Of course, Captain. I hope to hear from you soon."

They stepped off the turbolift and headed for the shuttlebay.

"Nuanka?" Chakotay asked as they walked. "You'll

have Fortier and his people rattling off our chants in no time at this rate."

"It's appropriate," said Sekaya. "A *nuanka* is a time of mourning, and that is precisely what these people are undergoing."

"You really do seem to have developed a rapport with them," said Chakotay as they continued on their way to the shuttlebay. "You're a natural as a spiritual adviser."

"Thanks. It's hard, though," Sekaya admitted.

They got into the shuttle. As they settled in and Chakotay ran through the standard readiness checklist, he said, "We have some private time here, as we approach the planet. I really want to hear what you have to tell me, my sister."

She didn't look at him, but nodded her agreement. "All the signs are present that assure me that you should be told. And for so bitter a thing, it will not be long in the telling," she said.

He looked swiftly, searchingly at her. Her hands were balled tightly in her lap.

"*Shuttlecraft Carrington* to *Voyager.*"

"Campbell here, Captain."

"Requesting launch permission."

"Permission granted. Shuttlebay doors opening. You are cleared to launch, *Carrington.*"

"You have to request permission? You're the captain," Sekaya said as the mammoth doors of the shuttlebay slowly opened, revealing a velvety field of black space and white stars.

He shushed her with a gesture and continued. "Readying launching sequence Alpha Beta Four. Launching."

Smoothly, the small craft lifted itself from the floor of the shuttlebay and moved forward.

"It's just standard procedure," Chakotay told Sekaya. "Everyone, from an admiral on down to an ensign, needs to obey it."

"Tradition," she said softly. "Ritual."

"If you want to call it that," he said.

He didn't want to prod her any more, and when he glanced over at her he saw that her eyes were closed. She opened her mouth and began to chant. The hairs on the back of his neck lifted at the familiar words, which he recognized although he could not fully understand or speak them himself.

At last, she opened her eyes and stared out first at the stars, then at the planet that was rapidly approaching. Anxious as he was to investigate the *chamozi* he had seen on the planet, Chakotay was more anxious for Sekaya to finally reveal what had happened to their people.

"You have never shown me what is in your medicine bundle, brother," she said.

Chakotay was surprised at the comment. "No," he admitted. "Would you like me to?"

She shook her dark head. "It's not necessary, but I have a question. Among the items you consider precious to you . . . is there a stone from the river?"

Of course, Chakotay thought. *She probably kept hers too.* "Yes," he said. "Given to me by someone very dear to us many years ago."

"I have a stone from a lake in mine," she said, her voice taking on a dreamy quality. "Given to me by someone very dear to us many years ago."

Chakotay tried hard not to be impatient, but time was passing quickly. "Sekaya, what does Blue Water Boy have to do with this?"

She turned to him and smiled slightly. "I see that sometimes you still do not possess patience. Bear with me. Everything is tied to everything, Chakotay. You toss a stone into a lake, and the ripples spread far and wide.

"We had every hope that the Cardassians would not interfere with our lives," Sekaya continued in a calm, steady voice, seeming to change the subject. He realized she was describing the events to him as she would tell a story around a fire at night: the great stories, the ones that lasted for thousands of years. This one, too, he suspected, would be remembered.

"And at first, they did not. . . ."

Kolopak entered the hut and removed his hat, running his fingers through his thinning hair. His wife, Tananka, and his daughter exchanged glances.

"More Cardassians."

Sekaya's words were a statement, not a question. The drum she had been working on so intently a mo-

ment ago lay still in her lap. Her father nodded and took the glass of water his wife offered him and drank deeply.

"I thought Gul Evek assured Anthwara and the council that they would not interfere," said Tananka.

"He did," said Kolopak. He stared at the glass in his hand. "Gul Evek is not here now."

Sekaya looked down. Normally, she enjoyed making drums, and was known for her skill. Now the hollowed-out segment of wood and the soaked rawhide skin seemed dreadfully unimportant to her.

"What is it they want?" asked Tananka.

Kolopak did not answer at once. Sekaya's gaze roamed over his increasingly agitated features. Kolopak was a deeply spiritual man, a man of peace. But it was clear he did not like the ever more frequent visits of the Cardassian conquerors.

"They want us all back in one place, first of all," he said. "They say it won't be permanent."

"What do you mean?" asked Sekaya. "We are already all in one place. No one has left the colony, ever, except—"

Abruptly she stopped and wished the words back. Even now, it was uncomfortable when anyone mentioned Chakotay. But her father seemed too distressed to notice—a clear sign of his inner turmoil.

"They want those who have moved away, to the plains or the river valleys, to come back to the original settlement site," Kolopak continued. "They have told *us that we must open our homes to those who are staying here."*

"That's not a problem," said Tananka. "We're of different tribes, but we have more that binds us than separates us. We can make room."

"But why do the Cardassians want us to do this?" Sekaya persisted.

"They told the council they simply want to know more about Dorvan V and its people," Kolopak said heavily. He did not sound as if he believed the statement even as he uttered it. "They are taking . . . inventory of their latest acquisition. They are making lists of all plant and animal life and doing some testing. They want all of us to report to have tests done, and it will be more convenient for them if everyone is in the same location."

"Tests?" yelped Sekaya. The rawhide and the ties were drying out. She did not care. "Father, what sort of tests are they talking about?"

"They appear to want to inventory us as well as the plants and animals," said Kolopak. His eyes flickered over to his wife. She met his gaze evenly, then turned back to preparing the meal. "Find out what blood types we are. Examine our cell structure." He waved a hand. "They told us in detail, but I have forgotten."

Sekaya stared. Her heart lurched in her chest and her stomach was tight. "This is not good," she said slowly. "I do not trust these people, Father. We are no different from any other humans. Our DNA, our cells, our blood types—surely the Cardassians will learn nothing new from examining us. This makes no sense. They must have another reason for wanting to do this, a reason they are not telling the council."

"Sekaya, we will cooperate."

"Don't speak for me."

"You are my family, I will speak for you."

His words were sharp. She sensed he spoke so because he, too, did not think this a good thing. "The tribe looks up to us. We need to set an example of cooperation. They are not asking for us to surrender anything but a little of our time."

Stubbornly, Sekaya shook her head. "History is repeating itself," *said Sekaya.* "People from another place have come here, to our home, and are laying claim to the land and to us. They are rounding us up like livestock, shuffling us from the place where we want to be to the place where they want us to be. Maybe Chakotay was right to leave. Maybe his is the example we should follow!"

"Sekaya, you will not speak to your father so!" *Her mother, too, spoke harshly. Sekaya could almost smell the fear.* "If that is all the Cardassians choose to ask of us, we should count ourselves lucky. You know what they have done to other worlds."

"And what harm is there in knowledge?" *asked Kolopak.* "As you say, Sekaya, my child—they will learn nothing new." *He tried to smile teasingly, as if this were nothing at all.* "I think there is some bureaucrat somewhere who feels he does not have enough to do, and wishes to please his superior. Lists and data are always impressive to those who worship technology instead of the spirits."

Sekaya looked back down at her work. Once assembled, the drum would be a sacred thing. Its voice would be heard as the tribe's heartbeat. Her own heart was hammering in her chest, and the desire to craft the drum was gone. She knew her father was right about one thing—it didn't sound as if the Cardassians were asking for much, on the surface of it. What harm could there be in letting one's DNA be analyzed, painlessly donating some blood, submitting to a retinal scan?

But they were Cardassians, and as far as she was concerned, that meant they could not be trusted. The council had opted to believe that they would keep their word. The people of Dorvan V would submit to the indignities in order to keep their sacred pact with the land.

Chapter
20

"SO WE WENT, like good little sheep the Navajo used to herd back on Earth," Sekaya said, continuing the story. "And as we went, we told ourselves this: Had not our ancestors suffered far worse treatment on our mother Earth? This was no great thing the Cardassians asked of us. Every single man, woman, and child, right down to the infants, submitted to analysis by the Cardassians with good humor, without protest. And for a while, it did seem that this bit of cooperation was all they wanted. . . ."

"Sekaya, daughter of Kolopak, I give you greetings."

Sekaya's heart stopped beating for a moment, then resumed with a sudden speed. It had been years since

*she heard that voice, years since its owner had been
betrothed to a lovely young Oglala Lakota woman and
moved with members of her family to the plains. . . .*

*She didn't trust herself to turn around. She stood
knee-deep in the lake, soaking more skins for drums,
and trembled. Finally, she realized it would be rude not
to acknowledge him. She turned to face him.*

*He was even more handsome than she remembered.
The youth's face had lines on it now, laugh lines
around his eyes and mouth, but the brown eyes themselves were as deep and mysterious as ever.*

*"Sekaya, daughter of Kolopak, gives greetings to
Blue Water Boy," she said, and she knew her voice
sounded strained and breathy.*

*He smiled a little sadly. "Much time has passed
since we last saw each other," he said. "I am no longer
Blue Water Boy, but Blue Water Dreamer."*

*That's right, thought Sekaya. The Lakota sometimes
modified their names to reflect who they became as they
made their way through life. A man in his forties would
no longer be Blue Water Boy. It wouldn't be appropriate.*

*"It suits you," she said, unable to think of anything
else to say. Attempting to continue the conversation,
she said, "I assume that you and your wife have come
back as the Cardassians requested?"*

*His eyes grew even sadder. "Only I," he said. "My
wife was killed two years ago in an accident."*

"Oh, I'm so sorry," Sekaya said sincerely. "May she

walk in the spirit world." The words were traditional for her tribe; Sekaya wasn't sure what the Lakota would have said. She knew her old friend would understand.

"Thank you," he said. "I miss her a great deal. But yes, you are right, I have come when the Cardassians called like a faithful pet."

Now Sekaya felt a smile tug at her lips. "You don't like this either?"

"Who would?" Blue Water Dreamer replied. "But it is best to cooperate. It's not as if we don't know what the Cardassians can do to a world if they think it's going to be troublesome."

She sobered. "True," she said. "It is good to see you, nonetheless."

"And you," he said. "The years have blessed you. I think you are even more beautiful than I remembered."

She felt her face flush and turned back to her skins. "I have to tend these," she said. There was no sound behind her, and she thought he had gone. Then she heard the song of the flute, sweet and lovely, spiraling up to the skies. It lifted her heart and also had a touch of wonder to it, like the magic the spirits were said to work.

When he had finished, she asked him, "What song is that?"

He looked gravely into her eyes and said, "That is the song the blue water sings to the sky, who is reflected and held in its heart."

"Oh," said Sekaya, and then, "Oh!" as he continued to hold her gaze and comprehension dawned.

"But then, they came back again. And this time, they wanted more. They wanted to ask us questions. Subject us to various . . . tests."

Sekaya's voice suddenly went thick and she fell silent. Chakotay wanted to interrupt, to get clarification, but he held his tongue. Sekaya was telling a sacred tale, and to interrupt would be highly disrespectful. If he had questions, he could ask them later.

"Some of the tests were strangely simple. They asked us to think of things, and see if others could guess what we were thinking. They wanted us to try to move objects with the power of our minds. We laughed about these; foolish Cardassians, we thought. . . ."

Kolopak had not approved of Sekaya's dating young men outside the tribe when she was younger. But now, even he had to admit that his daughter was a grown woman. She had never connected with any man in the tribe, never felt drawn to anyone but the mystical Lakota boy with the flute. She said nothing, but she knew Kolopak noticed the fact that since Blue Water Dreamer's return, they did nearly everything together.

"Oh, and then he said"—*Blue Water Dreamer made his voice sound very deep and serious*—" 'Now, my boy . . . see if you can move the pebble with your mind!' "

Sekaya laughed as they pulled in the nets from the day's fishing. Bright silver fish flopped and wriggled. They would be eaten tonight at the Feast of the Full Moon, and what was left would be dried the old way for future use.

"Really?"

"Really," continued Blue Water Dreamer. "It was all I could do not to laugh. So I did what he wanted. I closed my eyes, I concentrated, and I imagined the pebble flying off the table—and lodging in his nose."

"Too bad it didn't work," chuckled Sekaya, smiling at the image. She would have liked to see a Cardassian with a pebble shoved up his nose. She wished she could be the one to perform the act.

The nets were safely in. They should be paddling to the next site, to pull up the next net full of silver fish, but neither one did. Blue Water Dreamer leaned forward and stroked her face. Sekaya looked up into his eyes, her heart pounding. He smiled, trying to appear bold and confident but succeeding only in looking as nervous as she felt.

"I am remembering," he said softly, "a time from long ago, when Sekaya and Blue Water Boy were young. When their playmate, her brother, left for a brave new world, and they wept together."

"I am remembering that too," Sekaya said. Great Spirit, she was every bit as shy and nervous now, a woman in her thirties, as she was as a teenager.

"I am remembering something they did there," he

255

said, "something that stayed in Blue Water Boy's heart even when he became Blue Water Dreamer."

She swallowed hard. "Sekaya has not forgotten." Summoning her boldness, she added, "In fact . . ."

She snaked her arms around his neck and brought his mouth to hers. And the kiss was just as sweet and powerful as it had been over twenty years ago. They kissed for a long time, until a fish flopped out from the net and landed directly on Blue Water Dreamer's feet. He jerked away, and Sekaya laughed. He blushed, then laughed too.

When their mirth had subsided, Blue Water Dreamer took her hands in his, running his thumbs over the work-roughened surface with a tenderness that made her tremble.

"Sekaya, daughter of Kolopak," he said quietly, "tell this man what offering would best please your father. This man," he said, tapping his chest, "would ask for the hand of Kolopak's only daughter in the way that most honors her tradition."

She couldn't breathe. She stared at him, and his face fell. He looked down, and suddenly she realized what he thought—that she was refusing him. No! Oh, no. Sekaya placed her hands on his cheeks and turned his face back up to hers, and his dark eyes brightened as he saw the joy in her face.

So she taught him the traditional chant of Asking, and told him that he needed to fashion a headdress for them both, and to bring the headdresses to Kolopak as *evening fell the following night. And then she kissed him again. And again.*

But Blue Water Dreamer did not come to Kolopak's hut as he said he would.

Sekaya and Kolopak learned the next day that he had never returned from a second "Cardassian experiment."

Chakotay's skin erupted in gooseflesh. "You told me Blue Water Boy joined the Maquis," he said. "That he died resisting the Cardassians."

"After a fashion, he did," Sekaya said. The pain was not fresh, yet grief sat plainly atop her beautiful, strong features. "He was the first to fall in this conflict. We considered him a warrior, dying for the cause as surely as his ancestors died with bullets in their chests, fighting to protect their lands. Blue Water Dreamer went to the Cardassians willingly, to keep the peace, to honor the land he loved. To buy a future . . . with me."

She wiped at her eyes. "Damn. I thought I wouldn't cry telling you this."

"It's all right, Sekky." His own eyes were wet. He, too, had loved Blue Water Boy; the Lakota was the brother Chakotay had never had.

Sekaya pulled her long, thick hair to one side and parted the shiny black mass with her fingers. Chakotay could see a zigzag of raised pale flesh. He gasped softly.

"What—" And then he knew.

"We chose to keep the scars," she said. "War

wounds. Evidence of our victory over our oppressors. It was after Blue Water Dreamer's death that Father joined with those who would rebel. We hosted Maquis on our world; kept them hidden; kept them safe. We committed acts of sabotage, but we chose not to take lives. We were not foolish enough for that. The Cardassian vengeance would be swift and terrible if they had a blood debt to repay."

"Sekaya," said Chakotay, softly, shaking his head, filled with a new sense of wonder and respect for his sister, "you amazing woman . . . why aren't you dead?"

She laughed harshly, and inwardly Chakotay shrank from the sound.

"Once the war broke out . . . the Cardassians just left. I guess their resources were needed elsewhere. They never came back, but they had done enough damage. Sixteen people either died or disappeared because of their experiments, and several dozen were killed while they were with the Maquis."

They were nearing the planet. Despite his keen desire to get a good look at the *chamozi*, Chakotay didn't want to hurry their approach. His mind was reeling from all Sekaya had told him.

His people had *not* been left alone by the Cardassians. Far from it. They had been taken and experimented on like laboratory animals from the old days of Earth. They'd been murdered for their cooperation, and had risen to fight their oppressors as their ancestors had.

And Chakotay had known nothing of this. Nothing.

"Why didn't you tell me?" he said, his voice harsh with pain.

"You were an outsider," Sekaya said. She sounded tired, as if the telling of this tragic story had drained her. "We talked about it, Mother and I and some of the others, and decided that we wouldn't lie to you about it. We just . . . wouldn't share that part of our colony's history with you."

Anger blazed inside him, then subsided to an ember. He supposed he couldn't blame her. He hadn't been there, to suffer through it as she had, to know that a childhood friend—and in his sister's case, a future husband—had been slain to satisfy the whims of a conquering people.

"Did you ever learn what they wanted? Why they performed the experiments?"

She shook her head. "No. Who knows, with the Cardassians? Maybe to implement new and improved torture devices. Maybe just to kill some time. But it is right that you knew, Chakotay. I know you've just been handed a big responsibility with *Voyager*, but even captains get to take shore leave now and then. Perhaps . . . perhaps you can come back home for a bit. I'll show you the Cave of the Dead. Where we honored those who fell." She swallowed and blinked quickly. "I made a special altar for Blue Water Dreamer."

"I'd like that," Chakotay said. He extended his hand, and she squeezed it and let it go.

"Now you know why I feel so close to Marius and

his people," she said. "I know a little something about the loss he's feeling. And now, you do too."

Chakotay cleared his throat. "We're going to be landing soon," he said. "And we can think about our tribe and its history in a brighter light when we try and figure out why that *chamozi* is down there."

Sekaya nodded. "This sounds good. I have had enough of sorrows connected with our people, my brother. It's about time we were able to share something positive." Her eyes gleamed. "Let's go see it."

Chapter

21

"OUCH!" Ensign Walter Merriman hissed through his teeth at Kaz's gentle probing. Even though Merriman had reported to sickbay immediately after his injury, his side was already beginning to bruise.

"Sorry," Kaz apologized. "Well, you banged yourself up good, Ensign. Two broken ribs, a broken clavicle, and . . . are these bite marks? Good heavens, man, what were you doing on the holodeck?"

As soon as the words left his lips, he put two and two together and figured out exactly what Merriman had been doing on the holodeck.

The ensign's face turned beet red. "Um, just a program," he said.

Kaz smothered a grin. From the evidence in front of

him, he was willing to bet that Merriman was running a program that involved Klingons—particularly Klingon females—and he'd relaxed the safety protocols. A lot.

"The safety protocols are there for a reason, Ensign," Kaz remonstrated as he set about repairing the broken ribs. "You'd do well to adhere to them in the future."

"Hey," protested the burly Merriman, "a guy's gotta work out his stress."

"Certainly," Kaz agreed mildly, encouraging Merriman to sit up. "I actively encourage vigorous and *safe* exercise. But stress is only increased if the, um, exercise climaxes, shall we say, in a visit to your friendly ship's doctor."

Kaz hadn't realized that humans could turn quite that shade of scarlet. Merriman hastily got back into his uniform, murmured, "Thanks," and left.

Abruptly, Kaz's amusement evaporated. He'd just participated in a double standard, and one he didn't like. Why did he find it amusing that Merriman had participated in a rough-and-tumble, slightly naughty, and perhaps sexual scenario on the holodeck, and yet was concerned about Akolo Tare? The obvious answer was that Tare hadn't been a willing participant in the "program." She'd been kidnapped, physically subdued and abducted in front of witnesses, and in all likelihood raped. If she'd programmed it that way, that would be one thing, but she had been assaulted against her will. And that could never be tolerated.

But what about the holograms in Merriman's program? Granted, Klingons weren't often assaulted against their will, but they certainly had no say in what they were programmed to do.

They're much simpler programs, reason and logic argued. *You don't ask the computer if it's feeling up to locating a crewman. You don't ask your diagnostic tools if it's okay for them to check a patient.*

But I asked Data's permission when we worked together, part of him stubbornly responded. *I asked the Doctor.*

He felt a slight pain in his temple. The inner dialogue was giving him a headache. He frowned; he really must be tense. He rose and went to the replicator, requesting a glass of water with lemon.

And see, you didn't ask the replicator to very nicely get you a glass of water.

"Okay," he said aloud, "enough of this." He realized his hand was trembling as he drank the water.

Phaser fire, screaming through the night. He ran as fast as his legs would carry him. Finally, he saw her, spared somehow in the midst of the destruction that rained around him. Vallia's Revenge. There were dozens of them already here and he breathed a quick gusty sigh of relief at the faces that turned to him. Javan, Kehl, Rakkial, M'Vor—beloved friends and their families who were behaving as good little Maquis children always did, their eyes huge with terror, but staying silent and obedient.

Staying alive.

With hands that were numb from clutching his phasers, Gradak entered the code. The door hissed open, and they flooded inside. He looked around, searching for more. It wasn't hard; Maquis were everywhere, desperately crowding to get in ships, get off the moon that had once offered protection but now was a deathtrap. . . .

Sudden, sharp pain brought Kaz back to the present. He stared at his hand. Bright shards of glass were covered with blood that slowly dripped down to the floor.

"Jarem."

The voice was calm, but a thread of worry snaked through it. Kaz shook his head. The name was familiar—

Because it's my name—

Memory rushed back to him, and he looked up to see Astall standing just inside the door. When she saw recognition in his gaze, she ran toward him, taking his injured hand gently in her long purple fingers. With as much care as he himself would have taken, she removed the glass shards and placed them on a tray, then reached for the autosuture. The lacerated flesh closed and the blood disappeared.

"What are you doing here?" he asked, his voice shaking. If she hadn't come in when she had—

"We were going to meet for lunch," she replied calmly. "Now, tell me what happened."

He licked dry lips. "I started to have a headache," he said. "I was thinking about something and I went to get a drink of water. Then suddenly I was back in the dream, except this time it wasn't a dream, because I wasn't asleep."

"A hallucination."

Sickened by the term, knowing it was true, knowing what that would mean, Kaz nodded.

She looked up at him with deep sympathy, her ears drooping. "I'm so sorry, Jarem. But I'm afraid I have to officially remove you from duty."

"No!" he cried. "There are steps we can take. Look, the mission's almost over. Once we're on our way back, I'll remove myself from duty—"

He was frantic, babbling. This was his first mission aboard this starship, under the captain he so liked and admired, and he was cracking.

Astall looked at him searchingly. "What steps?" she asked.

He gave her a grateful look and squeezed the hand that held his. "There are two options," he said. "One medical, one mental."

"Go on."

He released her hands and went quickly to the computer. Tapping the controls, he called up a visual.

"Isoboromine," he said. "It's an organic neurotransmitter that mediates synaptic functions between the host and the symbiont. If the isoboromine level is too low, the interphase between host and symbiont gets off-kilter. We could both die. I did a scan after we talked to Chakotay." He looked up at her. "While I don't want to admit defeat yet, I have no desire to endanger anyone on this crew."

Her eyes filled with tears. "I never thought you did, Jarem."

He gave her a grateful smile and continued. "The scan showed that my isoboromine levels are below normal. I'm not sure why or how—whether the levels were depleted because of our attempt to bring Gradak forward, or if Gradak has been intruding so insistently because my isoboromine was low. It hasn't approached dangerous levels yet. But after what just happened, I think I should do a second scan just to make sure. My point is, I can artificially control the levels of isoboromine. I can increase it."

"And therefore have more control over the relationship between you and Gradak," Astall said as she nodded her comprehension.

"Correct. I didn't do anything to adjust the isoboromine levels earlier because we weren't trying to avoid my connection with Gradak. We were trying to increase it; trying to bring him to the forefront."

"But we can't complete that right now," Astall said. "So the best thing to do is minimize his influence over you. Do you think this treatment will be successful?"

"In theory, yes. But if it doesn't work, I'm planning on pulling out the big guns."

She cocked her head curiously. "And that would be?"
He told her.

Chakotay set the shuttle down gently at the coordinates
that Ellis had given them. Though the continent was in
the northern hemisphere, the colony was located far
enough south that there was a hint of the tropics. He
breathed deeply of the rain-cleansed earth as he and
Sekaya stepped out. His first officer was waiting there
to greet them.

"Mmmm," said Sekaya, breathing deeply as Chakotay had done. "This is a beautiful place. The holographic program didn't quite capture it."

"The markings are a short walk to the northwest,
right over this hill," said Ellis. He was clearly not in the
mood to make polite comments about the environment.
'It sounded like you knew what these symbols meant,
sir. Did you recognize them? You mentioned something
about . . . Sky Spirits?"

Chakotay looked up at the cloudless blue sky. Mois-
ture still hung thickly in the air, glistened on the leaves
of the plants. But the Sky Spirits had stopped their rainstorms. They must have wanted Ellis to find this symbol, wanted him to contact Chakotay. How they knew
about him, Chakotay didn't know, but with the Sky
Spirit aliens, anything was a possibility.

"It looks exactly like an ancient symbol our people
have used for thousands of years," Sekaya explained as

they strode over a grassy hill together. "It's a blessing on the land. We call it a *chamozi*."

"A few years ago, while we were lost in the Delta Quadrant," Chakotay said, continuing the explanation Sekaya had begun, "*Voyager* came across the exact same symbol on a small moon. We discovered that there was an alien race who had visited Earth forty-five thousand years ago and who had genetically bonded with our ancestors. My tribe's term for them was the Sky Spirits. Until that point, I had always thought it just a legend, a myth."

"Our tribe has *lots* of legends," Sekaya said.

"The Sky Spirits—the aliens—were afraid of us because they had visited Earth a few hundred years ago and seen what had become of humanity."

"I hope you corrected their misconceptions about us," said Ellis, almost primly.

"I did indeed. I was in a position to tell the aliens we'd evolved quite a bit. But I have to tell you, Ellis, I'm very curious to find a fresh marking here."

"Perhaps some of the Sky Spirits have decided to come back to this quadrant and pay us another visit," Sekaya suggested.

"Who knows?" Chakotay said, grinning at her. To Ellis, he said, "Changing the subject, where is the rest of the away team?"

"I had them fan out in pattern Beta Four Three Four," said Ellis. "They'll be meeting us at the colony site in a few minutes."

They cleared the hill, and Chakotay got a good look at the stone bearing the *chamozi*. The stone itself was roughly circular, about three meters in circumference. On its red surface could clearly be seen the spiral and two dissecting lines. Despite his determination to be calm and detached, his heart sped up.

"This is amazing," breathed Sekaya reverently. "What a blessing, not just for the land, but for us."

"Truer words were never spoken," said Chakotay. "I'm glad you're here to see this, Sekaya."

In silence, they descended the hill and stood regarding the stone. After a moment, Ellis cleared his throat, disrupting the mood of near reverence.

"I took some readings, Captain," he said, "but I found nothing. Do you two want to examine the symbol while I try again?"

Ellis's words sounded like so much prattle to Chakotay's ears. All he wanted—all his sister wanted—was to get close to the *chamozi*. Both siblings were already stepping onto the stone's surface as Ellis spoke.

"That sounds fine, Commander," said Chakotay, hoping he didn't sound as annoyed as he felt. He and Sekaya now stood before the symbol etched in chalk. Chakotay knelt, as did his sister.

"Oh, Chakotay. How I wish our father could see this," said Sekaya, her hand pressed to her heart. Chakotay nodded. As one, as if they had planned it, the two children of Kolopak reached to touch the white chalk.

Light exploded around them. Chakotay cried out and arched his back in pain, then knew no more.

Chakotay awoke slowly. His head throbbed, and there was a strange dimness about his vision. His body ached and tingled. He blinked several times in an attempt to clear his gaze, slowly turning a head that felt as if it weighed a thousand kilos.

And stared at the body of Commander Andrew Ellis.

He tried to bolt upright, but slammed hard against the restraints he hadn't even noticed were fastened securely around his body at wrists, chest, and ankles. His heart racing, he looked around wildly, trying to comprehend what he was seeing in his still fuzzy state.

The room was dark and it was difficult to see clearly, but Chakotay finally realized what he was looking at. A stasis chamber. Ellis was in a stasis chamber. Craning his neck, Chakotay looked around the small room.

He was strapped to a bed. Beside him, still unconscious and also strapped down, lay his sister. Neither of them appeared to be injured. Ellis had company; there appeared to be at least five stasis chambers that Chakotay could see. The clear material set into the almost coffinlike pods revealed the ghostly, unmoving faces of humanoid males. One was an alien; Chakotay groped for the name of the species but couldn't come up with it. The others, including Ellis, were human Starfleet officers.

Memory floated back to him: standing on the stone,

regarding the *chamozi*. Then the bright light, the pain, and then . . . nothing. He looked back over at Ellis. Clearly, whatever had stunned Chakotay and Sekaya had also stunned his first officer. He wondered fuzzily why Ellis was in the chamber and he and Sekaya were strapped down on the beds.

But this was not how the Sky Spirits operated. They were peaceful, friendly. They wouldn't stun strangers and put them in . . .

Federation stasis chambers.

He was becoming more alert. Shapes he could not put names to a moment ago now had identities. The dim light glinted off glass, metal, and other materials, and Chakotay realized that they were in some sort of hospital . . . or laboratory. There was a great deal of equipment that glowed and hummed softly. Looking directly up, he saw the rough surface of a cave wall instead of the smooth walls of a building or a ship.

Underground, then. And probably still on Loran II. He heard a soft moan beside him.

"Sekky," he hissed, keeping his voice quiet. "Are you all right?"

Chakotay turned to look at his sister. She appeared to be uninjured, but she was obviously as groggy as he had been when he had first awakened. She blinked and tugged dazedly against her restraints.

"What happened?" Sekaya asked in a slurred voice.

"An excellent question," came a crisp, assured voice. "And one we'll be happy to answer."

Both Chakotay and Sekaya turned their heads toward the sound. Sekaya uttered a brief, strangled cry and began to struggle in earnest. Chakotay's own eyes went wide with the shock of recognition.

Standing in the doorway, a look of superior confidence on his gray, scaly face, was the infamous Cardassian scientist Crell Moset.

But he was dead, had been killed in a prisoner transfer accident several years ago, after the battle for Betazed. How could he—

"You!" shrieked Sekaya. She struggled futilely against her bonds, fury distorting her attractive features. "You son of a *bitch*!"

Still slow in comprehension, Chakotay realized only after a few seconds what her reaction meant. Sekaya recognized the Cardassian. Horror swept coldly through him as he realized that this was doubtless the scientist who had "experimented" on his people. This was the man whose orders had cost Blue Water Dreamer and other innocent men and women their lives. This was the man whose atrocities had slain countless Bajorans in the name of "science," and who had then moved to continue his work first on Betazed and then on Chakotay's people.

For his part, Chakotay recognized the Cardassian from a holographic simulation the Doctor had constructed aboard *Voyager* years ago in order to save B'Elanna Torres's life. The Doctor had chosen to permanently delete the program; he could not reconcile using this man's knowledge, obtained through utterly despicable means, even for good.

"Hello, Sekaya. I'm flattered that you recognized me." The Cardassian smirked. "I must have made quite an impression. No, no, dear, don't struggle, you'll hurt yourself and I'll have to sedate you."

"And that just wouldn't be any fun at all, would it, Chakotay?"

Another person had entered the small laboratory. Another person Chakotay recognized.

Commander Andrew Ellis.

Chakotay made a small noise of confusion, then glanced back over to the first stasis chamber that had caught his eye. No, he hadn't been imagining it. Andrew Ellis was still enclosed inside, face quiet, eyes closed.

Chakotay looked back wildly at the Ellis who stood, grinning, beside a mass murderer, trying desperately to comprehend.

"It wouldn't be any fun at all," said Ellis. And then, before Chakotay's shocked gaze, his features shifted, blurred, and rearranged themselves.

Rearranged themselves into those of a man Chakotay hated more than anyone else in the universe.

The Bajoran traitor Arak Katal.

"So good to see you again, Chakotay," purred the shapeshifter.

About the Author

Award-winning author CHRISTIE GOLDEN has written twenty-four novels and sixteen short stories in the fields of science fiction, fantasy, and horror.

She is best known for her tie-in work, although she has written several original novels. Among her credits are the first book in the *Ravenloft* line, *Vampire of the Mists,* a *Star Trek* Original Series hardcover, *The Last Roundup,* several *Voyager* novels, including the recent best-selling relaunch of the series, *Homecoming* and *The Farther Shore,* and short stories for *Buffy the Vampire Slayer* and *Angel* anthologies. Sales were so good for *Homecoming* and *The Farther Shore* that they went back for a second printing within six weeks of *Homecoming*'s publication.

In 1999, Golden's novel *A.D. 999,* written under the pen name Jadrien Bell, won the Colorado Author's League Top Hand Award for Best Genre Novel. Golden has just launched a brand-new fantasy series entitled *The Final Dance* through LUNA Books, a major new fantasy imprint. The first book in the series is entitled *On Fire's Wings* and was published in trade paperback in July 2004. Look for the second in the series, *In Stone's Clasp,* in summer 2005.

Golden invites readers to visit her website at www.christiegolden.com.

STAR TREK

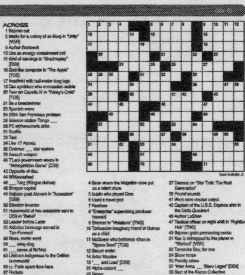

ACROSS

1 Bajoran cat
5 Medic for a colony of ex-Borg in "Unity" [VGR]
9 Author Stanbeck
13 Use an energy containment cod
15 Kind of carvings in "Shadowplay" [DS9]
16 God-like computer in "The Apple" [TOS]
17 Arachnid with ball-socket-bug legs
19 Dax symbiont who succeeded Jadzie
20 Tarer on Capella IV in "Friday's Child" [TOS]
21 Be a breadwinner
23 Spanish weave
24 2024 San Francisco problem
26 Science station Tango ___
27 PC alphanumeric abbr.
31 Saddle
33 Taxi
34 Like 17 Across
36 Omicron ___ star system
38 Assault weapon
40 T'Lanr government envoy in "Armageddon Game" [DS9]
42 Opposite of dep.
44 Whitewashed
46 ___ Targ (Klingon deshee)
48 Shogun capital
49 Bajoran poet Akorem in "Accession" [DS9]
50 Elevator inventor
51 Homeworld of two assassin sent to DS9 in "Basics"
53 Leader before Lenin
55 Aldoban beverage served in Ten-Forward
56 Mass. motto word
58 ___ wing-ding
61 ___ caves of Ne'Mat
63 Lifeform indigenous to the Oellen homeworld
66 1st. Paris spent time here
67 Redobs
68 Feredos commander who offered Kirk tranya
69 Klaang escaped from one in "Broken Bow" [ENT]
70 Cape for Scotty
71 Billiardi: Prefix

DOWN

1 Royal letters
2 Samaan friend of Jadzie Dax
3 Chess castle
4 Base where the Megedon once put on a talent show
5 Ndolo who played Qrex
6 Used a travel pod
7 Reecicen
8 "Enterprise" supervising producer Howard
9 Brenner in "Violations" [TNG]
10 Tarkossian imaginary friend of Chakoon as a child
11 McGivers who befriends Khan in "Space Seed" [TOS]
12 Serum ender
14 Actor Mccabes
18 "___ and Lease" [DS9]
22 Alpha-current ___
25 Server
27 Superstrona shout
28 Member of Klingon Intelligence in "Visionary" [DS9]
29 Regime on Exos in "Patterns of Force" [TOS]
30 Denellan creature Korax compared to Kirk
32 Fenad of Pi'Chan in "Survival Instinct" [VGR]
35 Mondernized
37 Deennat on "Star Trek: The Next Generation"
38 Pound sounds
41 Warp core reactor output
42 Captain of the U.S.S. Equinox also in the Delta Quadrant
45 Author LeShen
47 Tactical officer on night shift in "Rightful Heir" [TNG]
48 Bajoran grain-processing center
51 Kes is kidnapped to this planet in "Warlord" [VGR]
54 Tarcanche Baxy, for one
54 Show horse
55 Priestly robes
57 "Inter Arma ___ Silent Leges" [DS9]
59 Sect of the Kazon Collective
60 Miles O'Brien's coffee-cutoff hour
62 Of old
64 Gigekens. Abbr.
65 Fight finisher

Sam Batobis Jr.

STAR TREK CROSSWORD SERIES